I0718099

Melt: Snow Queen Retold

DEMELZA CARLTON

A tale in the Romance a Medieval Fairy Tale series

Lost Plot Press

ISBN-13: 978-1-925799-15-6
ISBN-10: 1-925799-15-8

DEDICATION

For all those who've found themselves singing
Let It Go
despite the desire to destroy that Disney DVD...
I feel you.

One

"Make way for the Sultan!"

Briska's heart stopped for a moment, before it started again, beating faster than before. No one noticed, for such a reaction was normal. Every woman in the king's harem undoubtedly experienced the same stuttering of her heart, because for every minor wife and concubine, a night in the Sultan's bed was a path to power, prestige, or perhaps a pretty present. Maybe even pleasure, if the Sultan liked the girl enough.

Not for Briska, though. It was fear, not anticipation, that quickened her heartbeat. For the Sultana had no need for more power or prestige, and her dowry had been such that it eclipsed the Sultan's own fortune, so she wanted for nothing gold could buy.

"Where is my queen?"

Briska allowed herself to smile, as her fear evaporated. Only one man called her that, in this land of strange titles and stranger customs.

"She is in her apartments, Your Majesty," one of the other girls said. "I will fetch her for you."

"No need. I know the way."

Briska smiled even more broadly. She carefully closed the door to her daughter's chamber, so that little Maram would not be woken by any sounds they made, before heading to the arched entrance to her apartments to greet her visitor.

He stepped inside, and she inclined her head. "Majesty."

He closed the doors behind him, shutting out the curious horde, before he lifted his head. Gone was the regal mien he wore for everyone else – he grinned fiercely and his face transformed from the cold monarch into the passionate lover she wished she could spend every moment with. "My queen."

She threw herself at him, her lips warming from his kiss as her body moulded to his, a prelude to a more intimate union once they managed to get their clothes off.

He tasted of wine and spices, kissing her as though he wished to consume the moment and make it a part of him forever. Then his teeth grazed her lip, drawing blood.

Briska gasped, her desire transforming into a spell that engulfed them both. He just laughed, as though he'd intended this all along.

He licked his bleeding lip – he'd bitten himself, too – and his magic came into play, far more powerful than her own. Her clothes vanished, and an enchanted breeze wafted across her skin, caressing her like the skilled lover who stood before her. The man who commanded the very air itself.

"I am yours," she whispered, letting the air currents lift her and carry her to the bed.

He stood at the end, surveying her, his eyes dark with desire. "Mine to worship," he said, kneeling on the bed between her legs.

The next breeze to caress her came from his parted lips, whispering inside her of all the magic he could work with merely his mouth.

And then words failed her, for the language they shared was one of touch and pleasure, until they both lay, satisfied and exhausted, in each other's arms.

"Mine to love," he said, pressing his lips to her breast.

"And I love you, Amani, as I have never loved any man before, nor will I, no matter what the future holds."

He drew in a sharp breath. "Not even…?"

Briska shook her head, smiling. "No, not even him. No one makes my body and soul sing as you do. Love has a magic all its own, more powerful even than yours."

He laughed softly. "The most powerful sorcerer in the world, a slave to love. And I would not have it any other way. But even a sorcerer must sleep, which I will not do in any bed I share with you, so I must leave you, my queen." He kissed her lips, the soft brush of goodbye, before he rose from the bed and cocked his head, listening. "Does the harem never sleep? It sounds noisier out there than when I arrived!"

Briska pulled on a robe, wishing she had the magic to be able to dress and undress at will, like he did. But she would never possess his power. "Perhaps one of the concubines has gone into labour. A few of the pregnant ones are close to their time. Heaven only knows why babies choose to arrive in the middle of the night. Why, even Maram – "

"Make way for the Sultan!"

For the second time that night, Briska's heart stopped with fear. A fear she would not give in to, as she drew herself up with all the fortitude of the queen she was. "Go!" she hissed, giving Amani a push. "Magic yourself invisible or – "

Too late. The doors flew open, and the Sultan stood beneath the arch, his stoic face revealing nothing but the cold fury of a man who knew no mercy.

Two

"For the Sultan's wife to bestow her attentions on any man but the Sultan himself is treason," the guard thundered. "Do you know the penalty for treason?"

That's the moment Briska changed from regal queen to pitiful heap, as she collapsed on the floor. "No," she whispered, staring not at the guard, but at Amani.

He met her eyes and said the words that should have given her all the courage she needed to stand strong once more. "I love you. My love for you shines brighter than the very stars in the sky, and it always will."

Instead, Briska burst into tears.

Armoured guards seized Amani's arms, dragging him out of the harem. Whispering women clung to each other, watching wide-eyed as he passed.

The Sultan had women aplenty – why did he need Briska? He could have just divorced her, freeing her from a marriage neither of them wanted, so that she might love the man she did want, but the Sultan was too selfish for that.

Accusing her of treason said he intended to execute her. Fire erupted in Amani's breast. Amani would not allow it. Was he not the most powerful enchanter in the world? He would save her even from the stupid Sultan. Her fool of a husband.

"Unhand me," he ordered the guards.

At least, that's what he means to say, but the moment he opened his mouth, one of them stuffed a wad of cloth in, then tied a second piece of cloth around his mouth so he could not speak.

Or bite his lip to draw blood to fuel his spells.

The most powerful enchanter in the world, rendered impotent by a rag that smelled…probably even tasted…of camel dung and sweat.

Then someone hit him over the head, and he knew nothing.

Three

"Leave us," the Sultan commanded. He waited until they were alone in the room before he held out a hand. "For heaven's sake, Briska, take it, and get up."

Unwillingly, she grasped his hand – colder and harder than Amani's ever were – and rose to her feet. "What do you want?" she asked coldly. He'd make it clear since Maram's birth that he wanted nothing else from her.

"The truth." He surveyed the room, as though looking for a suitable throne from which to deliver justice, but Briska's apartments were a place of leisure. If he wanted to sit, he could sit on one of the floor cushions. That would seat him lower than her. He sighed. "The guards tell me they saw a man who looked like me enter the harem several hours ago. But the midwife didn't see him, as she was busy with the mother of my son, so she sent a messenger to my quarters, telling me about the boy's birth. So when a second Sultan appeared…the guards knew there was something amiss. Tell me the truth. Did he come to you as me? Did you think…?" There was a yearning in his eyes, the like of which Briska had not seen for years.

Perhaps the fool still felt something for her, after all. A fool who had just ordered the death of the man she loved.

"The moment the doors closed, he revealed himself as the only man I could ever love," Briska snapped, feeling a spark of satisfaction as the hope in his eyes died. "Even without magic, he's ten times the lover you ever were. I begged him, many times, to do away with you and take your place as Sultan, so that I could be his wife in truth, but he was too honourable to break his oath to you. And now he will die at your hands, not because he was a traitor, but because he was too loyal."

His shoulders slumped. "If you say he tricked you, I could still save you, Briska. Nothing will save him, but you…"

She shook her head. "I would rather die with him, than live forever as your wife, knowing I will never see him again. Summon your executioner and take off my head, like I know you want to." She tried to make the words sound brave and forceful, pushing them out as a shield to hide the yawning pit of despair where her heart had once beat for joy. Never again. "You want the truth? I tricked him. Cast a spell on him, so he would fall in love with me. If anyone's a traitor, it's me, not him. Take me. Arrest me, and let him go." Hope blossomed within her. If she could save Amani…

The Sultan laughed. "Even if it were true, I cannot do it. If I let a traitor go unpunished, it will only embolden others. No, he will die a traitor's death, but you…I don't want to see you die, Briska. He must…but you can still live."

"I will not betray the man I love," Briska returned.

The Sultan sighed. "Very well." He raised his voice. "Send in the courtesan!"

Then he began to mutter under his breath. The words sounded like the ones she'd prayed to hear more times than she could count, but…why now?

The door cracked open and a woman sidled inside, then flung herself face-first on the floor. "Your Majesty."

His regal mask had returned. "Rise."

The courtesan – for that was what she was – sprang to her feet with more grace than Briska expected. Her face was veiled as though she'd come from outside the palace, but the gossamer thin silk hid nothing, allowing anyone to glimpse her golden skin and perfect curves through her translucent clothing. Why, Briska could see her peaked nipples clearly through the cloth.

The Sultan did not seem to care. "This is the enchantress, who confessed her treachery. She used magic to commit treason against me." He pointed at Briska, not even deigning to look at her any more. "I respectfully submit her to the justice of your people."

Your people. Panic flooded through Briska and she bit her lip, desperately trying to cast a portal that would take her to safety. Away from the fate worse than death that awaited her if she stayed.

The courtesan merely smiled and waved her hand, freezing Briska so she could no longer move. "Her magic is weak, this enchantress. One wonders how she thought she could succeed in her betrayal."

Now Briska wanted to tell the truth – that she hadn't bespelled Amani at all, until she knew his love for her was as strong as hers for him. It was no crime to increase a desire they already shared. But her mouth was closed, and she could not open it. Could not even sink her teeth into her lip for another drop of blood to cast a spell, any spell, that might help her.

A servant came in, carrying a mirror, which she set on the table, before she bowed and retreated.

The courtesan placed a ringed hand on the mirror's surface. "Now we may start. Your Majesty, a drop of blood?"

She drew a dagger from her belt and held it out, point-first, to the Sultan. He touched his finger to the tip, leaving a bead of royal blood.

She swiped her ring across her hand, leaving a shallow cut behind. The ring's jewel seemed to glow red through the layer of blood coating it.

"Kneel," the courtesan commanded, and Briska was forced to obey. "Now lift your chin."

Briska held her breath as the dagger came closer and closer, ready to slash her bared throat. The courtesan's gleeful smile was the last thing she'd see. Better than a lifetime of slavery as a queen or a…

The dagger pricked her, just above her collarbone, then retreated.

NO! Briska screamed in her head, but she didn't make a sound. She couldn't.

The courtesan touched her blood-dipped dagger to the ring, then leaned on the table. "By the blood of the ruler you betrayed, I bind you in servitude, djinn. By your own blood, the blood of a traitor, I bind you in servitude, djinn. And by my own blood, the blood of the judge who names you guilty of crimes against your ruler, I bind you in servitude, djinn."

Tears sprang to Briska's eyes and fell, unchecked, for she could not even blink them away. The courtesan had turned her into a djinn, a slave, forced to obey her master for eternity.

"Do you want her?" the courtesan asked the Sultan.

He shook his head. "As my Sultana, by my side, I would have given her anything. Now, she is nothing to me." And he said the words Briska had wanted to hear for so long, but now it was too late. "I divorce you, Briska." Three times he said it, until the marriage was void. He looked at the courtesan. "I beg you, take her away from here, and do whatever you want with her. I never want to see her again. See to it, Mistress Kun."

Briska couldn't even exclaim her horror. Slave to a courtesan? She couldn't imagine a worse fate. Having to share a bed with the clumsy Sultan had been bad enough, but a courtesan took dozens of lovers. If she commanded Briska to give herself to a man, any man, as a djinn she could not refuse. She would have to endure…

The courtesan lifted the mirror, so Briska could see the misty surface. Blood marred the frame where the courtesan had touched it, but the surface gleamed in the lamplight. "Look closely, for you will need this in my service," the courtesan said. "You may move now."

The force holding Briska upright vanished as quickly as it had come, flopping her forward in a deep bow. "How may I serve you, Mistress?" The words were out of her mouth before Briska could stop them.

The courtesan smiled. "Oh, you will be of great use to me."

"I am not very skilled at entertaining men, Mistress," Briska said. "Or at magic. The only man I ever seduced against his will just divorced me." Oh, how she wished she could have done things differently on her wedding night. He'd sworn not to consummate their marriage until she was willing, but she'd cast spell after spell at him until she forced him to take her maidenhead. A clumsy, painful encounter that she'd endured every night until she knew she carried Maram.

Maram. What would happen to her now?

"My daughter. Maram," Briska choked out. "What will he do with her?"

The courtesan stared at her. "You mean the Sultan? Is she his?"

"Of course. Amani did not come to court until after she was born."

The courtesan said, "Then the girl belongs to the Sultan. She will stay, but we must go."

"Where?"

Mistress Kun smiled. "Wherever I command you to."

"I am not very skilled – " Briska began again.

"Then you will learn to become so. Oh, not at entertaining men. No, you're going to do some matchmaking for me. Up in the Southern Isles, a daft name for such a northerly place, if ever I heard one."

"I have never…"

Mistress Kun snapped her fingers. "Silence!

Bring the mirror, and come with me." She opened a portal and stepped through.

Briska had no choice but to follow.

Four

"It's time to meet your first match," Kun said.

Briska blinked, staring at her mistress's image in the glass. The mirror sat on a natural shelf on the cave wall, as though the gingerbread-like rock had been baked by ancient hands in readiness for this day. Perhaps it had. Who knew?

Kun's face faded, to be replaced by a vision of a beach with two bodies on it. Two wet bodies, that looked like the waves had brought them reluctantly to shore but longed to reclaim them, licking at them tentatively before swallowing them forever.

"You must do everything in your power to bring these two together. The fate of a kingdom rests on this match," Kun said. "And so does yours, for if you serve me well, you may yet win your freedom."

The mirror clouded over again, shrouded in thick mist like the island outside, most days. Not today, though – today the rain poured from the sky without cease, soaking Briska to the skin as she dashed toward the beach. And the bodies.

Well, she couldn't match dead bodies, so they had to be still alive. Or her task would be over before it began. Briska wasn't sure what happened to slaves who failed to obey orders, but she knew it couldn't be good.

The mirror had showed the truth – a boy and a girl lay on the beach, in danger of being dragged out to sea if she left them there.

Briska headed for the boy first, for if she could wake him, perhaps he could carry the girl to the shelter of the cave.

But no amount of shaking or shouting roused him, so Briska dug her hands into the folds of his sodden tunic, and proceeded to drag him up the beach, out of reach of the waves. The wet weight of him nearly pulled her arms from their sockets, he was so heavy, but she managed to drag him about a yard before she had to stop to catch her breath. One yard….two…three…until she had him above the high tide mark.

Her arms hung by her sides, feeling heavier than the boy had, but Briska still had the girl to save. At least the girl would be lighter than her husband-to-be.

If the waves didn't get her first.

Briska hurried down the beach, gasping as a wave broke against her knees, sending freezing water swirling around her legs. She grabbed the girl, fighting the sucking sea as the wave retreated, until she emerged, victorious, on the wet sand.

By all that was holy, how could the girl be heavier than her husband-to-be? Her thick skirts dragged along the sand, catching on rocks and doing their best to hinder Briska as she heaved the girl up onto the rocks beside the boy.

If ever she needed magic to help her, it was now, but all Briska wanted to do was lie down beside the pair and rest for a week. But between her chattering teeth and trembling limbs, the freezing wind and her wet clothes, she knew she had to get inside…and so did these two.

Briska's hand drifted down to the dagger at her waist – a bone-handled thing with a stone blade so shiny it resembled green glass. She'd found it in the cave, echoing faintly of magic long since cast, so she'd claimed for her own. Briska ran her finger along the wicked edge. Blood mixed with salt water on her skin, and she tried not to hiss in pain as she turned her attention inward…to the magic that rarely came even when she called. A portal, she needed a portal to take her to the cave.

Briska traced a circle in the air, over and over, but nothing appeared. She fell to her knees and wept, but still her hand circled, blood dripping down her arm and staining her sleeve. Finally, she gave up. It seemed her enslavement had extinguished whatever little magic she controlled.

Time to do this the hard way.

When her task was finished, then she could rest.

Briska seized the boy, and began dragging him home.

He gave a strangled shout and struggled free.

Briska cried out and dropped him. His head clunked against the stone and he went limp, out cold once more.

Oh, by all that was holy…if she hadn't panicked, he might have woken and carried himself up to the cave. Maybe even the girl, too. Now she'd have to do all the work herself.

Swearing softly, Briska resumed her labour. Cursed by love and doomed to serve until she made the match Mistress Kun wanted. If only the Sultan could see her now.

Five

The girl woke first, despite the fever in her blood that sent wisps of steam rising from her clothes until they dried.

Briska approached the girl cautiously, knowing the lattice screen between them would offer her some protection if the girl lashed out. For who knew how these barbarians would react? What she'd seen of crusaders at home had demonstrated they had little honour, and these two looked no different.

"How are you feeling?" Briska asked softly,

but the girl didn't seem to hear her.

The girl grimaced as she sat up, holding her head as if it hurt.

Briska was no healer, but she could prepare tisanes for pain and fever. She slipped away to find some herbs to help the girl.

The girl's voice called her back with a question Briska could not quite make out. Yet when Briska returned, the girl's attention was on the cave furnishings…and her mistress's mirror.

A mirror in a place so backward they didn't know how to make glass, let alone a mirror.

The girl's eyes turned to Briska, full of knowing. "Let us out. I must go home." The barbarian girl drew herself up to her full height – a head higher than Briska – and stared down for all the world like she was a queen herself.

A slave she might be, but Briska did not have to obey this order. And she could do queenly better than this girl. "We all want to go home, but not everyone gets what they want. The sea wanted to take you from the beach where I found you, but I rescued you from the waves and brought you here. I must keep you two together. The mirror insists." Briska stepped out of the shadows, letting the mirror's misty glow light up her face as she tried to appear every bit the queen she once was. "Who are you?"

The girl shivered, her courage fleeing with her fever. "I am Gretel." She pointed at the unconscious boy. "That's my brother, Hansel." She kept speaking, but Briska didn't hear the words.

Brother and sister? Kun couldn't mean her to make an incestuous match like this one. Perhaps she intended to keep her here in exile, unable to make the match.

"Who are you?" the girl demanded.

Briska eyed her with dislike. "Once a queen, now a slave, loved by two men, one of whom is now dead and the other is dead to me. I am Briska, now queen of a rock that boasts little more than fearless deer and this horrible stuff called snow."

Forever cursed to be queen of this rock.

"You must let us go," Gretel insisted.

"I must do nothing of the sort." The words came out of Briska's mouth automatically, but even as she pressed her lips together to stem the flow, still the words repeated in her head. She must serve her mistress.

Then what of the mirror? Did she have to serve the mirror, too, or could it be wrong?

Haltingly, Briska continued, "The mirror says...the mirror says you must be together. But if you are brother and sister, as you say...then I am cursed!" The cursed queen of this rock, forever. "Bah, I should have known escape was an illusion." She tried to imitate Kun's superior tone: "You shall not leave here until you break the curse!"

Tears sprang to her eyes, and Briska hurried away, before Gretel could see her weakness.

Six

Briska waited for the girl to go back to sleep before she dared to use the mirror to contact Mistress Kun again. Even then, she took the mirror outside to use it out of sight of the pair.

"What is it?" Kun asked in irritation. Though Briska could not see below the woman's shoulders, she could see enough to know she'd roused the woman from bed. Briska would wager Kun had been pulled from a lover's arms instead of a dream, for Kun was too alert to be newly woken.

"You have made a mistake. They are not a

suitable match at all, but brother and sister. Hansel and Gretel are their names. Mistress, to make these two fall in love would be an abomination." Briska stuck her head inside and eyed the sleeping pair on the other side of the lattice, another of Kun's gifts. Kun had provided her with a modest bed, cooking utensils and a book to instruct her in using them and the spices from home, though djinn didn't need food, sleep or warmth. She had to appear like a normal human to these northern barbarians, apparently. As if a queen, albeit an exiled one, was anything close to normal. "I will not make this match!"

Kun's eyes flashed. "You serve me, and I order you to make this match. Do you hear me, djinn?"

"Yes, Mistress," came out Briska's mouth, unbidden. Before her tongue could betray her again, she hissed, "I hear you, but I will not!"

Pain erupted in her head, like nothing she'd ever known before.

"Welcome to your enslavement. As long as you refuse to obey, the pain will worsen. Obey me, and it will fade as if it had never existed.

Make the match," Kun said.

Blinded by pain, pressing her head to the stone floor in a desperate attempt to alleviate the agony screaming from one ear to the other, Briska was barely aware of the mirror returning to mist once more before she lost her senses to the darkness.

Seven

Shouting dragged Briska back to consciousness – the boy this time: Hansel. Her head only throbbed now, as though she'd drunk too much wine, but it was enough to make the shouting excruciating.

"Silence, boy!" she said, biting her lip and wishing she could cast some sort of spell to at least quieten him. But her magic was good for only one thing, and she refused to cast a seduction spell over the brother or the sister.

So she was forced to endure the sound of his voice as he cajoled her endlessly to let the two of them go.

Nothing he could offer her would be worth the knowledge that she'd be responsible for the abomination of an incestuous union.

Then he said words that held their own magic: "I shall build you a palace fit for a queen."

Grudgingly, Briska conceded, but only if the boy vowed never to share his sister's bed.

He didn't even hesitate.

The moment the promise left his lips, it seemed that the throbbing in Briska's head lessened. She had no idea why, but she wasn't going to question that now.

If the boy built her a palace, he would be too busy to have time to spend with his sister.

Eight

Briska's headache faded some days, only to rage with a vengeance the next, as Hansel sawed and hammered and built what the barbarian boy called a palace. The mirror flashed pictures of the pair, sometimes as they were at that moment, and sometimes locked in a lovers' embrace, as if to taunt her. But if Briska so much as thought her defiance at allowing such an abomination to happen, it was like Kun had buried a dagger in her head.

Briska took to carrying her dagger around with her everywhere, the cold stone a measure of welcome relief when her head pounded too hard to bear. She just had to lay the flat of the blade across her forehead and the pain receded.

A grunting, scuffling sound summoned her back to the cave, and Briska feared some strange creature had invaded her home. But what she saw was far worse – the mirror showed the pair naked, writhing in ecstasy in some cave that looked nothing like this one.

Briska's gaze darted to the lattice, but the girl was nowhere in sight. How had she escaped?

Briska drew her dagger. "It will not happen! Incest is against nature!" Not even the blade was enough to block out the agonising stab of pain behind her eyes. She fell to the floor, the knife slipping out of her fingers. She had to stop this. She had to. Her hands closed around the knife hilt, and Briska fought to find the strength to stand. "Better to kill them than let him defile her so. Now, before it is too late!"

She headed out of the cave, scanning the island for the entrance to the other cave, the one hiding the pair from her.

Pounding from the roof of the timber cottage drew her attention. The boy perched on the roof, whistling as he hammered one of the wooden roof tiles into place. He was fully clothed. There was no sign of the girl, either.

Briska stood watching him, not sure what to make of it. Had the mirror showed her a lie? Or had she imagined the image? No, surely not. She hadn't imagined the sounds they made. She'd never seen a couple so rapt in one another as they twined together. Not even with Amani had she ever been so…abandoned to everything but him.

Lost in thought, it took her a moment to realise the boy had climbed down, and now stood before her, holding the door open.

Hansel bowed extravagantly. "Your new palace, Your Majesty."

Some palace, but perhaps this cottage was a palace to these barbarians. Briska accepted his invitation, and made to step inside the house.

Gretel screamed something, then came running. She was fully clothed, too.

An invisible force slammed into Briska, throwing her against the door and holding her there. Magic. It had to be. Magic so powerful there was nothing Briska could do against it. She scraped her hand along the blade, desperately trying to cast a portal, but she could not even lift her arms against the force holding her in place. No portal, no escape…

"Don't you dare touch him, you bitch!" Gretel roared. Flames erupted from her hand, formed into a ball, then flew toward Briska.

Helpless to stop the missile, Briska was forced to watch as the ball of fire arced up, then down again. She prayed it would miss her, landing harmlessly on the ground.

The ball landed a foot in front of her, then bounced. This time, it landed on the toe of her boot.

Briska screamed and ran.

Too late. Her boots had caught fire, and a wall of flames surrounding her, allowing her no escape.

Unless she could cast a portal.

Blood dripped down her fingers, and Briska raised a shaking hand to trace a circle in the air, an archway through which she could pass. Pass, and live. Or burn and die.

Briska closed her eyes and wished.

When Amani woke, he was afraid someone had stuffed him into a chest and closed the lid. Or a coffin. They'd neglected to tie his hands, though, so it would be but the work of a moment to take off his gag, and cast a spell to make them rue the day they'd been born.

He tried to lift his arms, but they were squeezed so tightly between his body and the walls of his prison, he could not get even one hand free.

Wait…did he smell lamp oil? They couldn't burn him alive. Only barbarians did that.

He tried shouting through his gag, floundering in his coffin – it had to be a coffin, if they were going to burn him – but no one answered.

He heard the scrape of something rasping along the outside of his prison.

Amani tried shouting again.

It felt like a giant hand seized him, feet first, dragging him through a narrow opening that wasn't wide enough for his body. Tighter…tighter…crushing him…squeezing him into an impossibly narrow space where he couldn't breathe, couldn't feel anything but pain and pressure, couldn't even scream…

And then he was out, exploding into a cloud as the pressure was gone.

It took a moment before feeling returned to his arms and legs, and he was surprised to find his ribs didn't hurt despite definitely being crushed only moments before. Magic. It had to be.

But his hands were free now, free to untie his gag so he could spit out the foul-tasting cloth. The cloud around him cleared and he saw a man.

Not just any man. The Sultan, Briska's husband.

With a snarl, Amani opened his mouth to hurl every insult he knew at the man.

But what came out of his mouth was: "How may I serve you, Master?"

Amani tried to curse, but he only repeated the same words again. Furious beyond reason, he tried to strike the man, only to feel his body bow in deep respect for the man he hated.

He fought it, but his back bent anyway. The only bit of him he managed to keep from bowing was his head. He met the Sultan's gaze with all the fury he could muster.

"I don't want you to serve me at all. I never want to see your face again. Not after you stole her from me," the Sultan said.

"She was never yours!" Amani gasped out, before his own lips silenced him.

"But if not for you, she might have been, in time," the Sultan said. "Which is why I can't bear the sight of you."

Only now did Amani see that the Sultan held a lamp in his hands, a common thing of tarnished brass.

"So you may serve me by returning to the prison from whence you came, and sinking to the bottom of the ocean, where I will never have to look upon your traitorous face again," the Sultan said. He lifted the lamp high, then dropped it into the well. "I said go, servant of the lamp, and trouble me no more."

Amani didn't understand.

And then…he did.

His body crossed the paving stones in three strides, then dived into the well, head first, following the lamp. Amani hit the water, his strangled shout turning to bubbles in the blackness as he sought the lamp, compelled to follow. It glowed blue in the darkness, floating along in the current instead of sinking, calling for him to follow.

Not knowing why, he swam to catch up, stretching his hand out to grab the lamp. Only…his hand shrank, slipping inside the spout of the lamp, followed by his arm, until the narrow hole swallowed him up, scream and all.

Ten

Briska stamped out of her boots, but the blazing leather had already set the floor alight. Swearing, she bit down hard and fought to cast the only spell that could save her. The circle of blue light flared and died, once, twice…but on the third time it seemed to stay, wavering a little, but enough. She stepped through the portal, which collapsed behind her. She peeled off her singed stockings, to find her feet red and blistered with burns. She stuck her feet in the water bucket, moaning as the icy water numbed the pain.

The mirror unclouded for a moment and a face appeared. "Well done," Mistress Kun said.

"What do you mean, well done? That brother and sister almost killed me!" Briska snapped. This matchmaking thing was a lot harder than she'd thought. And incest...no, that hadn't been part of the bargain.

The woman laughed. "Brother and sister? You are too easily persuaded. That's what got you into this mess in the first place, but I will help you. This pair are matched, and so you will move onto your next quest. Your new assignment is in the icy north, I'm afraid. You will need warmer things."

Ice and snow? Perfect for burned feet.

Briska lifted her arms. "I am ready when you are, Mistress." The last word came hard for a woman who had once been a queen, but she had little choice now. Slavery to the mirror and its mistress was all her life held now.

A portal opened before her, and Briska stepped through. The mirror, her chest of belongings, and her precious sack of spices landed in the snow behind her.

Another day, another couple. Though she

shook her head when she thought of Hansel and Gretel. That pair would not have an easy time of it, she was certain. She might have made a match of them, however unwillingly, but they had a lot of work for even a hope of happily ever after.

Her mistress's face appeared in the mirror. "Next, you must match Kai and Gerda," she said.

Briska sighed as she saw the picture of the pair. At least these two had clothes on, unlike the fornicating brother and sister. Thank the heavens for small mercies. And snow to cool her feet.

From queen of a kingdom to queen of the snow, Briska's work was never done.

But first, she would need a place to live, for her new palace was gone. And all the ice and snow gave her an idea…

Eleven

Briska took a deep breath and then exhaled on the mirror. When the condensation from her breath faded, Mistress Kun's face appeared. "Mistress, I can't help but feel this is terribly wrong. I drove my sleigh through town, as you commanded, and just as you said, I stopped when the reindeer could go no further, and found a boy near frozen in his own sled, hooked onto my sleigh runners."

"Is he there with you now?" Mistress Kun asked eagerly.

Briska frowned at the boy, as still as a

corpse in his icy bed. "Yes," she said slowly. "But I should really take him home, for his family must surely miss him. I've put him into an enchanted sleep, which helps preserve him a little in this icy cold, but I'm not sure how long I can keep him that way, or whether it will do untold harm to do so. He's cold to the touch, barely draws breath…"

Kun waved her hand airily. "If you tried to take him home, he would undoubtedly freeze to death anyway. He has no family, no one who cares, except the girl he was trying to impress when he fastened his sled to your sleigh. Once she starts to miss his company, she will come to claim him. But if you do not, she will not yet care…and you will have to find another way to make this match."

Briska wrung her hands. "But if anything happens to him…I can't make a match if the boy's dead. And it's a dangerous journey up the mountain alone. All sorts of things might happen to the girl before she gets here."

Kun laughed. "The girl will not be alone, for she'll have plenty of help. You're not on that lonely rock any more, with nothing but deer.

You just concentrate on keeping the boy there, ready for when she arrives."

"But…"

"That is an order."

Briska slumped. "As you wish, Mistress."

"If you tire of watching him, then perhaps you can make a new match while you wait. Lubos and Molina, a prince and a miller's daughter…"

Briska stared at the unlikely pair, wondering what could attract a prince to some common peasant. Oh, she was pretty, she supposed, but not unless she stretched out naked before him, at precisely the moment when he fancied a roll in the hay…

Men. So predictable. She would have this pair so tightly entwined with one another not even the king himself could break them apart. And before Kai woke, too.

"Yes, Mistress. I will match them, too."

"Good. Watch out for Rumpelstiltskin, though, for he will try to stop you at every turn."

Briska opened her mouth to ask for more information, but it was too late. The mirror's surface returned to a reflection of the icy walls of the palace. Only then did Briska curse the day she'd ever agreed to become a djinn. A prince and a peasant, some man with a strange name, plus this frozen boy and a girl intent on rescuing him…Briska could feel it in her bones: neither match would not turn out well for her, at all.

Twelve

Daily, Briska asked her mistress about the progress of the girl who was to save the increasingly pale boy in her palace.

"She is travelling down the river by boat."

"She has been captured by a witch."

"She seeks word of him from flowers."

"Some crows have taken her under their wing."

"She is at the royal palace, sleeping in the prince's bed."

Each answer seemed worse than the last.

"If she has become a prince's mistress, then

surely she will not want the boy. May I send him home?" Briska asked, reaching out to touch the boy.

"Of course not. She merely sleeps in his bed. The prince has a wife of his own, and shares her bed. The girl mistook the prince for her match, the boy you hold, and you must keep him still, for she will come for him. She will be along shortly, for she will soon meet the reindeer who pulled your sleigh, and the beast will bring her to you."

Then the mirror clouded again, before reflecting the wall.

Briska should have felt relieved, knowing the match would be made soon, but she couldn't shake off an awful feeling of foreboding. After all, that Hansel and Gretel pair had seemed like such a simple match to make, and they'd nearly killed her.

Curse that Gretel girl for hiding her powers. What kind of witch did such a thing? Why, the girl deserved to be a djinn for misusing her powers so. It was only a matter of time before she came to the attention of her king, and what monarch would want a fire witch free in his kingdom?

The sooner the better, really, for if the girl found out Briska had survived the blaze…Briska shivered, and not from cold.

And here she was, waiting for what had to be another witch to arrive, for Gerda must have some magic in order to speak to plants and animals.

Dread settled in Briska's belly, like she'd swallowed a stone. She had to wake the boy, and take him home. No, take him home, then wake him.

A portal. She needed to cast a portal, the kind of magical doorway that would let her travel from here to his home.

Briska bit her lip, praying she could cast it this time. She traced a circle with her hand, then another, and another…

Over and over, she sank her teeth into her lip, until all she could taste was blood, but the portal never opened. Briska fell to her knees, defeated, and let her tears fall. Only they tinkled as they hit the icy floor, frozen the moment they left her face.

With the temperature dropping, both she

and the boy would need more blankets. If they could not leave, then they must endure…and wait for the inevitable.

Thirteen

The moment Briska saw the reindeer outside, she looked for a place to hide. But where did one hide, when every wall of her palace was made of crystalline ice, so clear you could see through them?

So she left the boy in the chamber with her mirror, and hid in the farthest corner of the palace from him. For hours she huddled in her corner, waiting for the couple to leave.

Finally, when it was dark enough outside for the aurora to be seen, she crept from her hiding spot. The light played across the walls, spinning and fracturing and reforming around her, but Briska ignored it. She would use the mirror to contact her mistress and tell her the match was made, and then –

Something crashed into the back of her head, sending her tumbling to the floor. Briska's hands scrabbled for purchase on the frozen floor, but she found none. The best she could do was to turn herself over to face her attacker.

"That's the witch who bespelled me," the boy said, pointing.

The girl hefted an icicle in her hand, a deadly point as long as her forearm. "What did she do to you?"

Briska scrambled back, skidding on the ice until her back met the wall. "I didn't do anything. I didn't, I swear!"

"She cast some spell on my sled so I couldn't unfasten it from her sleigh, and I couldn't get off, either. Then she cast some other spell on me so I couldn't move, and dragged me here to freeze to death. There's no other food here. She must mean to eat me!"

"No, I – "

The girl advanced. "We can't let her live. If she planned to kill and eat you…how many others has she murdered already?"

"Please – "

The boy stretched out his hand. "I should strike the blow, not you, Gerda. After all, it was me she meant to kill."

Gerda held the icicle out of his reach. "Get your own and we'll do it together. I'll watch her, and make sure she doesn't try anything." She turned her glare on Briska.

For the second time, Briska found herself facing a witch who wanted to kill her. Why hadn't she been gifted with more than a whisper of magic power? The only spell she knew she could cast would only make her situation here worse, for the one thing this girl desired most was Briska's death, and Briska could only heighten that desire, not change it.

"Please, I mean you no harm. Just take your friend and go," Briska pleaded.

But Gerda was deaf to her pleas.

The boy returned, carrying an icicle as thick as his arm and easily a yard long.

Briska's voice died. She could only look

from one to the other, begging with her eyes.

"On three," the girl said grimly.

"One, two…three!"

Briska screamed as two ice spears drove into her body. Something warm gushed down her back and she dimly realised that one of the spikes had gone right through her.

She slid to the floor, her vision fading.

The last thing she saw was the boy and girl, lifting the mirror between them to smash it on the floor, before they walked out of the palace, hand in hand.

Briska's last thought was that at least she'd made the match right before she died. Mistress Kun couldn't fault her on that.

Fourteen

Rasping again. Amani tried to shout for whoever it was to stop, but the only sound was a gurgle, for there was nothing but water in his cramped quarters. How he was still alive, he did not know.

Then the horrible feeling of being squeezed and crushed came again, before Amani drew in the most beautiful breath of air his lungs had ever tasted.

"How may I serve you, Master?" he boomed, ready to reward whoever had freed him from his tiny prison.

"It talked! The lamp smoke talked!"

Amani found himself facing two shabbily dressed camel drivers, one of whom must have dropped the lamp when he fell backwards in surprise. The two men ran away.

Amani sighed. He allowed himself the luxury of looking around. He was no longer in the Sultan's palace, judging by the desert dunes on all sides of the tiny spring. Definitely outside the city gates. He had no idea how much time had passed. A day, at least, for the sun was sinking and it had been night time when he was last forced into his prison.

He nudged the lamp with his foot. Such a tiny thing, but he could see the magic twining around it, and him, biding them together. Imprisoned in a common, tarnished lamp. The Sultan had truly intended to insult him. And he'd succeeded, curse him.

"Who are you?" an imperious voice demanded.

Amani looked up. The voice belonged to someone dressed as richly as the Sultan, or Amani himself.

"I am Amani, the most powerful sorcerer in

all the world," Amani said grandly. Hope swelled in his chest at the realisation that he hadn't been forced to bow to the man. Was he somehow free?

"He came out of this, Your Highness!" one of the camel drivers said, seizing the lamp. He shook the sand off it, then presented it to the well-dressed man.

"What was a powerful sorcerer doing inside a lamp?" the well-dressed man asked.

"I was imprisoned inside it for my crimes, Master," Amani said, hating the words that he could not stop himself from saying. "I am the slave of the lamp, ready to obey your every wish."

"Hmm." The well-dressed man eyed him thoughtfully. "I have no need of another slave, but if you are telling the truth about being a powerful sorcerer, perhaps I might find some use for you. Rejoice, for you now serve Prince Philemon of Tasnim!"

Tasnim, the mysterious underground city that owed its wealth to its water wells, deep under the desert, that travellers paid a great deal to drink from. In better circumstances,

Amani might have offered his services to the Prince of Tasnim. But he could not rejoice, no matter how strong the order. Some magic was beyond even Amani.

For without Briska, life could hold no joy.

So he said, "Yes, Master," and waited. For what, he did not know.

Fifteen

Briska blinked her eyes open, barely believing she could. "Is this paradise?" she asked.

"Heavens, no. If paradise were this cold, even the virtuous souls would have revolted by now. I'm sure it's as fitting as fire is for hell. Hardly a reward."

"Mistress," Briska managed to say as Kun's face came into view. "Why am I not dead?"

"Don't look to me for miracles. You're a djinn. You can't die. No matter how many holes that ungrateful pair punched into you."

Briska coughed, then doubled over in agony

as the movement set fire to her chest. She reached to touch her torso, feeling for the holes that were no longer there. "How?"

"I pulled them out. Then your body simply healed, like djinn do. Enslavement isn't all bad when it includes immortality." Kun shrugged. "It's supposed to be a punishment, prolonging the period of servitude. You don't age and you don't die. Some djinn have lived for centuries."

Centuries of this? "Better to die outright than to suffer it over and over again."

Kun regarded her. "You are allowed to use your magic to defend yourself, you know."

"My magic is not strong enough for that."

"After the fire and now this, I wonder what use your magic is at all." Kun hung the mirror back on the wall, which appeared to have never been broken. "Perhaps I should have just left you here, impaled on ice."

Briska moistened her lips. "Thank you for saving me, Mistress," she said. "If you give me another chance, another couple, maybe…but not a witch. Djinn or not, I do not think I can survive another spell."

Kun laughed. "Who do you think you are

matchmaking, if not witches? Someone must see that another generation of magic users is born, and tend the bloodlines. Every match you make is for a witch."

Briska shrank against the floor, wishing she could sink right through it. "Then help me hide from them, Mistress," she begged. "I will make the match, cast what spells I can to help love blossom between whoever you command, but please hide me from them. If there was some way I could stay here, far from harm, and still bespell them…"

"Perhaps there is," Kun said, stroking the mirror. "But you must promise to match every couple I send you, without protest. There shall be no repeat of the Hansel and Gretel affair."

Briska shook her head, then winced. "No, Mistress. I shall match every couple." That Gretel girl still gave her the shivers. "Is there any way you can hide me from Gretel, too?"

"I shall cast a spell on the mirror, allowing you to use it to not only see the couple you are to match, but cast spells through the glass, too. And I shall hide this palace, so that no magic may find it. All you must do is stay within its walls, and you may hide from the world. And I will not have to come here to save you again."

Briska lay back, breathing a sigh of relief. "Thank you, Mistress."

Some time passed before Kun said, "There. It is done. On the morrow, I will send you a new couple to match. Take care that you do not let all the ice up here freeze your heart, so you can't even cast your feeble love spell."

Without waiting for an answer, the enchantress cast a blinding blue portal and vanished.

Only then did Briska dare to breathe again. Her heart had frozen the day Amani died, and nothing would touch it, ever again.

And love spells? No one could cast those, not even the most powerful enchantress, for love had a magic of its own that overpowered all other spells. No, she worked with lust, and seduction. She could seduce a man to her bed in a moment, or stoke a spark of lust into a raging inferno. If that Hansel and Gretel hadn't been brother and sister, she'd have matched them the moment they woke in their prison. As for Gerda and Kai…

Briska swore she'd do better next time. And if she was safe in her icy citadel, far from the reach of any vengeful witch, Kun would never have the excuse to call her spells feeble again.

Sixteen

"Enough," Briska commanded, and the writhing, naked bodies in the mirror turned to reflected blue. Now she was done with them, no one would pry Snow White away from her prince.

She pressed her hands against the icy wall, then against her flaming cheeks, attempting to cool them. The glassy walls were weeping, it felt so hot in here, almost as though the steamy scene between Snow White and her match had heated up the palace, too.

If Briska had Amani here right now, she

would…

She closed her eyes, feeling the icy chill invade her heart again. She didn't need to look to know the palace had frozen into its usual crystalline splendour, showing no sign of the recent melt.

Mistress Kun would be pleased at her success, she was sure of it.

If only Briska could feel some measure of satisfaction in it, but she felt nothing. While passion raged between Snow White and her prince, her heart was empty.

There was no one left to love.

Even her daughter had been torn from her.

If she could only see Maram again…

Briska stretched a hand toward the mirror, wishing with every bit of her being that she might glimpse the girl again.

But Maram was too young for matchmaking. She was barely old enough to play with the dolls Amani had bought for her.

The mirror surface rippled, clouded, then cleared.

Briska's breath caught in her throat.

Maram crouched in the garden, unnoticed in

the dark. Light and laughter floated from the harem halls, but Maram only hugged her dolls tighter to her chest. What was the girl doing, awake so late? Had no one put her to bed, as they should?

Women passed her, taking no notice of the child.

Briska bit her lip, sending a spell through the aether to the harem. She let it expand like mist, until it had touched every woman present.

"Where is Maram?" murmured one, then another, until the whole harem started searching for the little girl.

It was a concubine who found her, a girl Briska remembered because she'd borne the Sultan a daughter not long after Briska had birthed Maram. What was her name again? N-something. Naheed, that was it.

Briska dug her teeth deeper into her lip, and sent out the most powerful seduction spell she'd ever cast. Not at Naheed but at the little girl in her arms.

A chorus of coos from the women standing around Naheed told her the spell had worked.

"Yes, love my daughter for me," Briska said. "He might have removed me from her life, but she will not go unloved. Every one of you will hold her as dear as your own child."

She watched greedily as Naheed hugged the girl tightly, carrying her to bed. Briska would have given anything to hold Maram in her own arms, and perhaps one day she would, but in the meantime…she would at least watch.

As long as her mistress never found out.

For Kun must never know.

Briska took one last, longing look at Maram, before wiping the picture from the mirror. She would tell Mistress Kun about her success with Snow White in the morning, and accept her next assignment. One day, the matchmaking would end, and Kun would release her to go home to her daughter. One day.

However long it took, however many matches she had to make, Briska swore she would win her freedom.

For Maram.

Seventeen

A dragon. A huge, fire-breathing, sword-crushing dragon. Briska stared in awe, hardly daring to believe her own eyes. Giants, unicorns…she thought she'd seen everything with this couple, but she hadn't expected to actually see a dragon.

It should have been simple, but she'd learned by now that no witch's mind was simple. George had needed barely a nudge from her magic to fall madly in love with Melitta, but the cool, collected maiden didn't seem to experience passion of any kind.

And when she did…Briska had thrown the spell so hastily she'd been responsible for breaking three beds before she realised the lust in Melitta the mindreader's mind was from someone else's thoughts, every time. She'd almost gotten them killed once, when the lust had belonged to a giant. But lust came in many forms, and a man maddened by battle lust became a liability.

So she'd followed their journey, day after day, hoping to find that tiny spark in the girl's mind she could fan into a flame.

If the dragon didn't burn everything into ash first. Disgusting, destructive beast. His lust for killing hung like a black cloud over its head, almost obscuring it from sight. A cunning creature, but if she could bespell him so that his battle lust outweighed his reason…her pair might have a chance…

She watched in horror as the battle raged, fire and smoke obscuring all, until a scream rose up that could only have come from Melitta.

Briska hunted desperately for the girl, but even the mirror could not find her among the flames. George had disappeared, too. If the dragon had killed him…or both of them…Briska had failed.

She slumped against the wall. She'd never hold Maram in her arms again.

The mirror had gone awfully quiet, aside from the crackle of flames. Too quiet for a battle.

"Marry me."

Briska jumped to her feet, hardly daring to breathe. Had she heard correctly?

When George kissed Melitta, Briska pumped her fist and cheered so loud icicles fell from the ceiling, but she didn't care. Her couple were alive and kissing and…she bit her lip, shooting a spell their way. Alive and kissing and Melitta had every intention of dragging George to bed with her that very night. If she didn't throw him down into the ashes and tear his clothes off then and there…

"Another happy couple, and a dead dragon to boot. There's nothing feeble about that, Mistress," Briska said.

For the first time in she couldn't remember how long, she felt a grim sense of satisfaction.

It was gone before she could grasp it, but it was there, nonetheless.

Perhaps she could win her freedom. After beating a dragon…anything was possible.

Eighteen

If anything was possible, then she could make the mirror show him, Briska told herself for the dozenth time. No, surely the hundredth. But this time was different. This time she reached out to touch the mirror as she breathed on the glass. And wished, more than anything, to see Amani.

The mirror fogged, like always, and Briska held her breath, not daring to take her eyes from it. Her heart pattered in her chest, almost as fast as her footsteps would sound as she ran to Amani, if she could see him again. Touch him again.

The fog cleared, but the picture was blurred. Blurred by her own tears at the thought of seeing him again. Tears of joy, Briska told herself, blinking them away before they froze.

Somewhere…blue. The rush of water, like when she'd ducked her head under the surface in the bathhouse while her servants were filling the bath. The slight tink of metal hitting stone, like one of them had bumped the bucket against the side of the bath. But not the hollow ring of an empty bucket – whatever the metal thing was, it was full of water.

Her heart leaped. If he was in a bath, he certainly couldn't be dead. As soon as the mirror cleared, she would see his fine form, and…

The mirror surface shimmered, and Briska closed her eyes, taking a deep breath before she dared look.

At what turned out to be her own, disappointing reflection.

No Amani. No bath. Just her own pale face, in front of the palace wall of blue ice.

Had she just witnessed his death? Had they

drowned him?

Her legs refused to hold her any more. She fell to her knees and wept, not caring if her tears froze this time, for each tiny crystal drop would only reflect the ice silencing her heart.

Nineteen

Days passed, each the same as the last. She would spend weeks making a match, and only then would she permit herself another glimpse of Maram. Most days, she managed to resist temptation, but the very darkest days were made darker still by her failed attempts to see Amani in the mirror.

She told herself every story she could think of – he was a powerful enchanter, unlike herself, and he could easily shield himself from spies, even those with magic mirrors at their disposal. He could have any one of a number of reasons for remaining hidden. But in her heart she knew the truth, for Mistress Kun had already told her: the mirror could only find the living, not the dead.

If Amani did not appear in the mirror, then his heart no longer beat for her, for the Sultan had surely silenced it forever.

On those dark nights, she would weep until she fell asleep, only to wake with her face a glittering mask of ice crystals from her tears.

Once the queen of a desert kingdom, now she was only the queen of snow and ice.

And her subjects…the latest couple were a stubborn pair whose affection for one another was clear, but who let duty and family get in the way. She longed to slap some sense into both of them, but she dared not leave her palace.

He was a warrior, a general who had killed more men than she could count. Prince Rudolf, whose luck in battle was legendary. Luck. Huh. It was all her, turning aside weapons at the last moment or bespelling his opponents. She could not match him with Portia if he died in battle.

And Portia…oh, she was as stubborn as he was. An uncrowned queen from the same islands as Hansel and Gretel, surrounded by a bodyguard of young men who would have turned any normal girl's head.

If she could get the two in a room together, it would be easy – she'd have them in each other's arms within the hour. But they were miles from one another, separated by not one but two armies, and an unforgiving ocean.

It might be years before they met again, and Briska could match them properly.

So she cheated. Every night, after making sure the pair lived through another day apart, she spent an hour watching Maram.

Maram slept near Naheed and her daughter Anahita, and the two girls were never far apart. When Naheed died, it was Maram who comforted her sister, and took care of the other girl, for the lowly daughter of a concubine was beneath the wives' notice.

Every night Briska watched her, she'd strengthened the spells on Maram until the girl's own magical ability surfaced, stronger than Briska's own. Maram was no enchantress, but her seduction spells were more powerful than even those cast by Mistress Kun.

No woman in the harem was immune to her charms, and nor was the girl's father. It placed her in a unique position. On the one hand, she was easily her father's favourite, but on the other, she was his daughter, and she would never be a rival for her father's nightly attentions with the wives and concubines. Thus, the women trusted her. She knew every secret they dared confide in no one else, and more than once she'd shared them with her father without ever betraying her source. Oh, not everything – just matters that might affect the wider court, and not mere harem matters. She'd inherited her father's talent for politics, something Briska didn't understand.

All in all, Briska was proud of her daughter. The girl was growing up into a most satisfactory princess.

Then Rudolf crossed the ocean, and went to war in Portia's territory. It was a good thing Briska did not need to eat or sleep, because keeping that pair alive while she waited for them to get close enough for love to spark took every moment of her days and nights. If it wasn't one, it was the other.

She wanted to scream at Portia that queens did not need to take up a bow in their own defence – that was what she had guards for! – but the chief of her guards was that horrible Hansel who'd almost been the death of her, so Briska didn't dare make her presence known. If Portia was anything like Gretel, who had also taken up the fight beside Rudolf…a barbaric people, arming their women, instead of keeping them safe.

Once she was done with these two, she vowed wearily, she would ask Mistress Kun for a simpler match to make. Love between a pair who fate had thrown together, or turning enemies into lovers, perhaps.

Finally, a night came where both Portia and Rudolf found a safe place to sleep, and Briska dared to direct the mirror's surface away from them to something other than those cursed Southern Isles.

For a moment, she considered searching for Amani, but decided against it. She wanted to see her daughter, for she hadn't seen the girl in weeks.

She took a deep breath, exhaling on the glass, then waited for Maram's face to appear.

Briska found Maram in tears, crying quietly into her pillow. Where was Anahita? Normally the other girl would be comforting her, but Maram was alone.

Briska cast a quick seduction spell over Maram, as she did every time she saw the girl, then breathed on the mirror again, willing it to show her Anahita. The girl hadn't looked ill the last time she saw her, but accidents could happen anywhere.

Come to think of it, she hadn't seen the two together for some time. If the girl was dead…

The fog on the mirror faded, and Briska held her breath as she peered into the picture it showed.

Briska's mouth dropped open, and wouldn't close. She wanted to look away, but her own horror transfixed her.

No one deserved such a fate.

Twenty

Amani squirmed, trying to find a comfortable position in the cramped lamp, but it was no use. Whatever magic held him prisoner in the piece of worthless metal wouldn't let him move. Not until someone rubbed the tarnished brass, when he would once again be sucked out the spout to do something stupid.

Like create a lake in the desert, where one shouldn't be.

He cursed his master silently, for such were the terms of his enslavement that he could not say the words aloud. Even if the Prince of

Tasnim was all of the things he couldn't say.

It wasn't Amani's fault the idiot had ordered him to make that lake. Princes didn't care if whole underground rivers had to be shifted to grant their wishes. Bedrock cracked…the desert would be forever changed by what he'd done. So when the prince had whined that he wanted everything changed back, Amani had taken great pleasure in informing the idiot that it was impossible. Not even the most powerful sorcerer in the world could force the river to flow backward.

Which was probably why he was stuck in the lamp again, with no way out until someone summoned him. He'd lost track of the days, he'd been in here so long. How did you count days when everything was dark, anyway? He had not eaten or drunk a thing, and sleep eluded him, yet these things no longer seemed to matter.

Djinn had no need of sustenance or sleep. They served, and they waited, until they served again. Slavery. On an immortal timescale.

And the longer he sat in this lamp, the more he longed for freedom. Even servitude would be a release from this lamp.

But he'd probably need a new master to do that. That new enchantress hadn't liked Prince Philemon much. Whatever curse she'd cast on him, he hoped it made the prince as uncomfortable as Amani himself. And unable to wish for any more stupid things.

Amani sighed. The next man who released him from his prison, he'd make the man the master of untold riches.

As long as he wasn't some puffed-up prince like Philemon.

Twenty-One

"Do you know what you have done?" Mistress Kun demanded, her eyes flashing even through the mirror.

Briska lifted her head from the cradle of her arms. "I cast too strong a lust spell on him. I know. I was trying to fix it or reverse it or something when he…when he…" Raped the poor girl. Briska couldn't say the words, knowing she was responsible for the brutal violation of the young enchantress. She buried her head in her hands. "The match is doomed now."

"Worse than that. You cast your spell on the wrong brother!" Kun snapped.

"What?"

"You cast the spell on Thorn, the older brother, when Zuleika is destined for Vardan, the younger one!"

"There's two brothers?" Briska didn't believe it. "Two identical brothers? But there is only the one in the palace…"

Kun made an impatient noise in her throat. "Of course there are. And they are not identical, just similar in appearance. The other is the new Master of Beacon Isle, a powerful post his fool brother let him have without realising the consequences. Now that he does, he'd planned to send your enchantress to carry a curse to his younger brother, but your misplaced spell made him change his mind and decide to keep her instead!"

"Perhaps I can reverse the spell. If he becomes indifferent to her, he might change his mind once more and send her anyway…" Briska ventured.

"It's too late for that. Your bird has flown far from Thorn and his kingdom. That enchantress might be young and just coming into her powers, but she can cast portals like she's been working magic all her life." Kun sniffed. "Unlike some people I could name. And why weren't you watching? You should have seen her leave and done something to stop her!"

Briska gritted her teeth. "I could not watch the king rape that poor girl. Not when I couldn't stop him. She's the same age as my own daughter…and what if her father decides to marry her to someone like that? She is a princess, and a suitable wife for a king…" She trailed off before she revealed her secret – that she watched Maram through the mirror most nights. "As long as I am distracted with worrying about my daughter's future, I will likely continue to make similar mistakes to the one I have with Zuleika and…what was the boy's name? Vardan?" Briska's breath caught in her throat. "What if Zuleika comes after me, blaming me for what Thorn did to her?"

"How many seduction spells have you cast?" Kun asked, but she didn't give Briska time to answer before she continued, "And how many of the men you have cast them on turned into beasts like that one and forced the girl?"

"Just him," Briska said, "but that doesn't absolve me. That girl suffered because – "

"Because you cast a lust spell on a complete arsehole," Kun finished for her. "The girl suffered, true, but she will have her revenge. A fitting one, for he will lose his throne to his greatest fear – his brother, or his brother's heirs. She was clever, too – she managed to curse him without committing treason, because he activated the curse. She will not become a djinn."

"But what if she comes here? She is far more powerful than I will ever be. And it's still my fault!" Briska said.

Kun waved away her worries. "She does not know of your involvement, and she is on the other side of the world now, helping some warrior woman with her magic shoes. She has put the matter out of her mind, and so should you. Even if she did not, she would not find you through the shields here. As long as you continue to make the matches I command, you shall be safe. What about that couple in the

Southern Isles?"

"Blissfully in love with one another," Briska said bitterly. "No spell required. After all those years of trouble, keeping them alive, I'm not sure even magic would have stopped those two once they were reunited."

"Really?" Kun looked delighted. "Even I didn't think you could manage to make that match. Well done. Such good service begs a reward. What would you ask of me?"

"Let me visit my daughter, and speak to her father about what marriage he has in mind for her," Briska said. And persuade him not to let her marry at all. Better for Maram to be celibate than suffer the same fate as Anahita.

Kun shook her head. "I cannot. He does not wish to see you ever again."

"Then ask for her to be your apprentice," Briska said. "If she is a courtesan, she will never marry, and if you train her, she will still be able to make alliances for him. Just not marriage alliances."

"You would sentence your daughter to a life without love?" Kun asked.

"There is little love in a political marriage,

either, without a spell to bring the pair together," Briska countered. "Better that she becomes a courtesan, allowed to take the lovers she chooses, than to be forced into a marriage she does not want, where to love a man – any man – would be treason. That is a life without love. I would not wish my fate on her."

Kun inclined her head. "Very well. Princess Maram shall be a courtesan. If she has inherited your gift for seduction magic, she could well become the best the world has ever seen."

"My daughter has no magic. Mine is so weak, and her father…if her father had been an enchanter, perhaps it would be different." If her father had been Amani…but that could never be. Briska swallowed, then dared to ask, "Is there anyone this mirror cannot show? Can I see my daughter? Or…anyone else?" She didn't trust her voice to stay steady if she said his name. The pain was too raw still.

"The mirror will show you anyone living. If you wish, once your work is done, you may use it to see your daughter."

Briska let out a breath she hadn't known she was holding. "Thank you, Mistress. It would be wonderful to see her again." Then Kun's other words sank in. "By living, you mean…if the mirror will not show someone, then they must be…"

"Dead," Kun finished for her. "Dead and buried, where no magic can touch them. Any other questions?"

"No. I…thank you for taking such care of my daughter. I will watch you eagerly," Briska said.

"And while I am training her…"

"I will fix the mess I made with Zuleika."

"No, not yet. Give the girl some time to recover from her ordeal or she will reject the brother. Instead…how about a pair of starcrossed lovers, childhood friends whose families are feuding? Jael and Halvard could do with some magical assistance." Kun waved her hand, and her reflection was replaced by a picture of a pair Briska had not seen before.

"As you command, Mistress," Briska said, bowing. "And thank you," she added softly.

As long as Kun kept Maram safe from

having a husband like Anahita's, or that horrible King Thorn, Briska would do whatever her mistress asked.

Twenty-Two

"She's a girl!" Briska wanted to scream at the conceited prince. Anyone with eyes could see Mai was no man. She moved with a dancer's grace, the slight swing of her hips betraying her on every step, but the illusion spell that made her look like a man blinded them all, especially the stupid prince. Too busy looking for his next opponent in the sparring ring, he'd barely spared a glance for the girl who Kun and her cursed mirror had declared were the man's perfect match.

He called the boys ladies, sneering around

the circle, and they all hung their heads, not wishing to fight him. All but her, because, by all that was holy, she was a lady, smaller than any of them. Still he did not see it.

A small maiden with a wooden sword, standing up to the bully prince who was easily twice her size. She showed no fear, no emotion at all, as she faced him.

Briska had watched him beat boy after boy, but she didn't want to watch him beat the girl. "She's a girl!" she repeated, as she cast seduction spell after seduction spell at him, but the only thing he lusted for was battle, and he charged at the girl, murder in his eyes.

She barely moved, but it was enough to take her out of his way and send him sprawling. The only bit of her out of place from his passing was her shoe, which the prince had evidently carried away with him in his charge. A magic shoe, glowing faintly purple with power.

Prince Yi did not see the magic, not even when he pocketed the shoe.

The more Briska watched the pair, the less she thought the prince deserved her. Mai moved like a hunting cat…or a hawk…or a snake…her sword darting out like an extension of her arm to block the prince's blows again and again until she tapped him on the chest.

The prince wheezed and doubled over, backing away. Evidently it had been more than a tap, or it had touched some vital part of him.

Seizing her chance, Briska cast a spell at the girl, hoping to inspire her affection, so that she would step forward and offer to nurse the prince back to health. Then, surely…

The clack of wood on wood echoed off the ice walls behind her, and Briska held her breath. Instead of offering to help the prince, the girl had continued to battle him. What manner of people were these two, whose only lust was for playing with swords?

She swore softly as she watched them battle on until the prince landed in the dirt a second time. There was passion between the two, definitely, but it was something more akin to hatred than love. For the moment, at least, she mused as an older man broke up the bout. As long as there was passion, she could work with these two. After helping the Big Bad Wolf catch the third Little Pig, matching a prince with a girl who lost her shoe would be easy.

97

Twenty-Three

When the prince finally returned Mai's shoes and asked her to become his wife, after no small effort on the part of Briska and even Zuleika, Briska allowed herself the luxury of another peep at Maram.

Her daughter looked much like Briska herself, for her enchanted servitude had kept Briska unchanging on the outside while she aged imperceptibly inside. Yet the years had aged Maram, too. Travelling to foreign courts and bewitching foreigners with her beauty and wit, all the while brokering trade agreements for the Sultan had turned the girl into a woman more worldly-wise than Briska would ever be.

The courts Briska observed in secret, casting spells through the mirror while she stayed safe in her palace of ice…Maram marched into with her head held high, the unchallenged mistress of all she surveyed. When she departed, she carried many new jewels and other precious gifts, most of which she sold or traded away at her next port of call. After one trading expedition, her wealth was more than her mother's dowry, making her the wealthiest woman in the Sultan's kingdom. Richer than the Sultan himself, Briska suspected, until the trade agreements Maram negotiated began to bear fruit. Maram would have made a formidable queen, and more than one foreign prince had offered for her hand, courtesan or no.

But no matter how eligible the offer, she had declined them all. Briska thought it was because none of them had yet managed to touch her heart. Because for all she'd inherited her father's political acumen, Maram was definitely her mother's daughter. It would take an extraordinary man to capture Maram's heart, though the girl would leave a trail of broken hearts behind her.

While her mother made matches between two people, Maram united entire nations. She had a courage Briska would never possess. Briska prayed that Maram would never need to know the violence that had driven Briska into hiding.

But today, as Briska watched the girl shrug out of her clothes in the old bathhouse by the city gates, she was struck by the deep sadness that seemed to surround Maram, a dark pool far deeper than the water she stepped into. For all her conquests, happiness eluded Maram, too, much as it had her mother. Was Maram destined to spend her life alone, in the midst of so many, yet untouched?

But she wasn't alone in the bathhouse, Briska noticed — a shadow lurked in the linen room, the shadow of a man, she was certain of it.

The mirror obeyed her order to focus on the man, to see which of her suitors was spying on Maram, and whether he meant her ill. But this man was no suitor Briska had ever seen before. His patched, worn clothes made him appear little more than a common beggar, until Briska recognised the make of them. A fashion from decades past, only ever crafted in silk, but worn so threadbare now she couldn't discern any of the original sheen. A nobleman or a merchant, fallen upon hard times…did he blame Maram for his misfortunes, and seek revenge?

Briska sent a spell through the glass, fanning the flame of his existing passions. If it was Maram he wanted, then he would make himself known to her instead of hiding. If it was revenge…better that he reveal himself now that her servants were alert for her call for aid.

The man edged out of the shadows and into the light, but only to where he could see Maram better.

Not a man at all. He was barely more than a boy, his father's cast-off clothes hanging off his thin frame, but the way he stared at Maram was like a man dying of thirst regarding a cup of wine. Infinite longing.

Briska reached through the mirror and sent a stack of towels tumbling off the shelf. The boy never heard it, for he was too intent on Maram, but Maram's head snapped up, as she became aware that she wasn't alone.

She summoned him, using the same honeyed tones she might try on one of her suitors. Unlike those other men, he crept out of hiding and prostrated himself before her.

Briska would have called for her attendants to take the boy away, knowing that the boy deserved death for invading the Sultana's privacy. But Maram, for all her regal airs, was not a virtuous queen.

She called for food to be brought, enough for two, claiming the man as a lover to her servants, though she'd only met him. She even honoured him by serving him with her own hands, something Briska had not even done for the Sultan himself.

The boy – Aladdin, he'd said his name was – was nothing and no one, yet Maram treated him like her equal. She offered him food, drink…and then she did the unthinkable. She offered him her hand, and he took it.

A look passed between them, for the most fleeting moment, but Briska caught it, for she knew it well. In that touch and in that glance, two hearts had connected. If only other matches could be made so easily.

Briska sent a seduction spell at the boy, the strongest she could muster, and instead of stepping closer to Maram, he bowed his head. Swearing softly, she cast a second spell, this time aiming squarely for Maram.

Love could spark, but sometimes it needed more to fan it into a proper, enduring flame.

"Kiss me," Maram said. What should have been a command came out as a desperate plea.

Quietly, Briska retreated, willing the mirror to return to mist, so that her daughter might enjoy the boy's heartfelt kiss in peace and privacy.

For the first time in more than a decade, Briska wanted to weep for joy. A man had touched her daughter's heart. One who might be able to give her the love she deserved. Love Maram might return.

Her heart considerably lighter, Briska lay back on her bed of ice, secure in the knowledge that while her own heart was frozen, at least her daughter's future would be happy.

Twenty-Four

Another day, another master…or the same one in a different guise, but it mattered little. One master was the same as another, issuing orders and expecting miracles. Amani braced himself for being sucked through the spout again. The discomfort had become one of the least demeaning parts of his servitude.

He placed a private bet with himself that this new idiot would ask for all the riches in the world before the day was over. He'd lost the wager when it was Philemon, who'd turned out to be too much of a fool to think of asking for such a thing. So this one would have to be truly stupid to do worse than Philemon.

"I am the servant of the lamp. What do you wish of me?" Amani said grandly. He'd found he could vary the words if he wished, as long as he said something suitable when greeting a new master. If he began before the magical compulsion hit him, he could even make himself sound impressive, retaining some of his former glory, instead of presenting himself as a cringing, servile mouse.

He found himself facing a peasant woman. One who backed away from him in terror, clutching the lamp in her clawed fingers.

She tripped and knocked herself unconscious, which brought a ragged boy to her aid. Now both of them were ignoring him.

So much for making a grand entrance. Amani sighed. "I said: what do you wish of me?"

The boy – nay, a man, though a young one, turned angry eyes on Amani. "You frightened my mother and now she is hurt."

Amani opened his mouth to say it was her own silly fault, releasing a djinn she had no idea what to do with.

But her dutiful son snatched up the lamp, and continued, "I wish you would fix the mess you have made." His expression challenged Amani to refuse. Almost as if he knew the horrible headache that would ensue if he did.

It had been many years since Amani had healed someone, but he did his best for the woman. When he had stopped her head from bleeding, he turned his attention back to the man. His new master, for the man's hands were firmly wrapped around the lamp as though he knew what power he possessed.

Grudgingly, Amani said, "What else do you wish of me?"

He would not blame the boy for asking for riches. Living in this hovel, a bag of gold might change his life.

But the boy surprised him again. "Answers. What are you?"

"I am the servant of the lamp, and my master is whoever holds it in his hands."

The boy nodded, as though he already knew this. "So you are a djinn?"

"Yes."

"You can perform magic? What sort of magic can you do?"

The boy had met djinn or enchanters before. He must have, for only people who knew magic well knew an enchanter's powers were strong in some areas and weak in others. If Amani had been able to render himself invisible, he would never have been caught with Briska and he wouldn't be in this mess. But there was no point thinking of that now — he had a new master to impress with the considerable powers he did have.

Amani swelled until his head touched the ceiling. "I can make you the richest man alive. Transport you to the farthest reaches of the Earth and back again in the blink of an eye. Build you a palace so magnificent even the Sultan will beg to see inside."

The boy was going to ask for riches. Amani could almost see it running through his mind. "What would you wish me to do first, Master?" Amani asked.

The boy considered the question for a long, long time. Finally, he said, "I am hungry. Bring me something to eat."

Amani stared at him. He offered him the world, and the boy wanted a snack? Though Amani had to admit he'd seen more meat on some skeletons. Perhaps the boy was wiser than he gave him credit for.

He bowed and left, determined to bring the boy a meal fit for a king. Amani grinned. Why, he'd bring him a meal fit for a Sultan, taken from the Sultan's own table. He could spare it.

Twenty-Five

Even in his lamp, Amani heard the name of Briska's daughter, Maram. He pressed his ear to the spout and tried to listen harder. How could this peasant boy know Princess Maram?

At first, Amani wanted to laugh at the irony of it all. It appeared his new master – Aladdin, his name was – had chanced to meet the princess in a bathhouse, and he'd fallen in love with the girl, much as Amani had fallen for her mother. Unlike Amani, though, Aladdin planned to marry the girl.

The Sultan would never let his precious

daughter marry some starving peasant boy. Amani owed it to Briska's memory not to let the girl fall into the wrong hands. Yet as he listened…it seemed the boy truly loved Maram. Whether Maram felt the same was another matter, though.

So much for asking for riches. The boy was about to ask for a love spell, and Amani had never been so happy at his own shortcomings. Even if he could cast such a thing, he could not cast one on Maram.

Amani emerged from the lamp, pre-empting the summons from Aladdin. He took a deep breath, ready to refuse the boy's command so firmly he never asked again.

Aladdin met Amani's gaze squarely, and asked for a palace.

Amani suppressed a snort. If it wasn't love spells, it was riches, always.

But as Aladdin detailed what were quite modest requirements, as far as palaces go, it dawned on Amani that he wanted the palace for Maram, and Maram alone, for Maram was marrying someone else.

Amani stared at Aladdin in wonder. How

could he be so calm, knowing the woman he adored would be another man's wife? What kind of man wasn't willing to fight for the woman he loved?

Amani hadn't stood by idly. No, he'd fought for her love and won it and…

…landed himself in his current predicament.

Perhaps there were better ways to go about winning a woman's heart, and her hand. For Maram was not married yet. And Amani owed it to Briska to see her daughter happy in marriage, as Briska herself had never been.

Amani bowed low before departing. He would build Maram a palace better than anything the Sultan had ever seen, and he would do everything in his power to find out where the girl's desires lay, and see that she had the husband her heart wished for. Whether it was the man she was going to marry or Aladdin or some foreign prince, it mattered not. He would grant the girl this one wish, for her late mother's sake. For she did not deserve her mother's unhappy fate.

Twenty-Six

It worked out better than Amani could have hoped. Briska lived, and her daughter would live happily ever after. Sure, Amani was still a slave, but he was happier than he could have hoped for. If he had to serve someone, Maram's new husband was hardly a bad choice, for he was a good man. If Amani told Aladdin how much Maram missed her mother, Aladdin might even order him to find Briska. One day, perhaps.

Lost in his daydream at what might be, Amani should have paid attention to Maram, who now stood with the lamp in her hand. His mistress.

Maram's eyes glowed, just like her mother's had when she attempted magic. But the power flowing through Maram was far more than Briska had ever commanded.

"Blood of the betrayed that binds this djinn, my father's blood that runs in my veins, too, will set us both free." Maram placed her bleeding hand on the lamp, smearing the stuff over the blackened brass. She turned her glowing eyes on Amani and threw the now useless lamp on the floor. "You are free. Find her, free her, and be happy."

It felt like waking up from a dream, a dream he'd believed was real. The fog lifted from Amani's brain, allowing him to think clearly for the first time in too long.

How could he possibly have considered himself happy, serving some peasant boy? Sure, the boy had honour and a good heart, and he'd won the heart of Briska's daughter, too, but that didn't give him the power to command the most powerful sorcerer in the world.

Amani considered the order Maram had given him, but he no longer felt a compulsion to obey. He truly was free. Free of his prison, free from slavery, but he would never be free of his debt to Maram.

So for the first time in his life, he willingly abased himself before someone.

"As you command, Princess. When I find her, I will tell her that you have found happiness, too. If you ever have need of me, you have only to call, and I will be there to grant your wish." He touched her hand, healing the cut she'd made to free him. Only then did Amani rise and incline his head to Aladdin, the man a moment ago he would have willingly served. "Enjoy your palace. Consider it my wedding gift to the princess. But if you ever hurt her…know you will incur the enmity of the most powerful enchanter in the world. A man with no master. Not any more." He bit his finger until it bled, then traced a circle in the air. The portal opened, as he knew it would, and Amani stepped through.

Twenty-Seven

Amani stepped out of the portal and sank up to his knees in sand. In his absence, the desert and the thick stone walls had kept his home secure, but he hadn't counted on the desert itself invading his castle. Perhaps because this was a war his servants had fought while he lived here, but now they were gone.

It mattered not. When he returned here with Briska to make the desert castle her home, she would help him choose suitable servants. In the meantime…Amani closed his eyes, summoning a magical sandstorm to blast his palace clean.

He surveyed the tiles, laid at the command of one of his royal ancestors. The same one who had ordered the mosaics and frescoes on every wall and domed ceiling, from which he'd taken his inspiration for Maram's palace. Modern art, created for one of these new religions that had invaded the region, could not compare to this. Four hundred years it had stood, and it would outlast these religious fanatics, he was certain of it.

And these ancestral walls would witness his triumph as he found the woman he loved, and brought her home.

Amani ensconced himself on the floor of the entrance hall, beneath the frescoes of his ancestors hunting, and closed his eyes to begin his own quest.

He bit his lip, tasting blood, then cast a searching spell, letting it spiral out over the desert, looking for his lost love.

He concentrated on Briska's beloved face, breathing deep and steady to keep his focus. The spell must find her. Over sand and water, mountains and plains, forests and fields, army camps and cities, his spell flew, searching for what he did not find.

But Amani would not give up. She lived – Maram would not lie to him about something so important. Unless the Sultan had lied to her, too…

Fury built as Amani's spell swept around the globe, finding nothing but emptiness.

Amani opened his eyes. Nothing could hide her from one of his search spells. Nothing. For who was more powerful than him? Only death could outmatch him. If death had taken Briska…

Then the world was no longer a place he wished to live in, either. But first he would exact his revenge on the man who had driven his beloved to her death.

Amani leapt to his feet, slashed open a portal, and strode through.

Twenty-Eight

Amani almost skidded on the tiles, he moved so fast, but he merely slowed to regain his balance before marching on. "Where is she?" he demanded.

The Sultan had aged twenty years and swelled as round as the world he wanted to rule, but somewhere in there was the bastard Briska had married before he enslaved them both. So much for the virile young leader, hungry for power and wealth, who had thrown Amani's lamp into a well. Now he'd eaten so many perfumed jellies he'd turned into one.

"Where is Briska?" Amani repeated, louder this time, as the quivering wreck of a man cringed away.

"I don't know!" the Sultan shouted back, his eyes bulging. He opened his mouth again, undoubtedly to shout for his guards.

Amani grinned. A wave of his hand slammed the doors shut, shrouding them in a bubble from which no sound could escape. "No one can hear us, and I will not leave until you tell me what you've done with her."

The Sultan's mouth opened and closed, like a dying fish. Amani had a brilliant idea.

"If you don't tell me where she is right now, I shall turn you into a fish, and I will sit here and watch you suffocate to death, drowning in air like you tried to drown me in that well." Amani seated himself on a bench and folded his arms.

The Sultan blinked, his fear fading. "Amani?"

Amani inclined his head. "The very same."

"You haven't changed a bit. You look just as you did the day you betrayed me." The Sultan jumped to his feet. "And as your master, I command you to open the doors, and get out of my sight!"

Amani grinned. "Ah, but didn't you hear? I am not a djinn any more. I have no master, for I am free, and my powers are greater than they have ever been. And it is you who betrayed her, for I know she begged you for a divorce so that she might marry me. You loved her money too much to release her, and look at all it has bought you!" He waved his hands at the palace walls, which he was happy to see were still inferior to Maram's mosaics.

"My wise rule, and my trade agreements have won me this wealth. Not some wife's paltry dowry," the Sultan snapped.

"You mean trade agreements won by the lovely Princess Maram, don't you? You whored Briska's daughter out to foreign princes while you sat here like a fat spider in his web, waiting for her to bring rich prizes to you!"

"How dare you insult my daughter!" the Sultan roared.

Amani flashed a mirthless smile. "I know the lovely princess well. You would have given her to that piece of carrion, Hasan. If not for me, she would not have lived long enough to marry her beloved Aladdin. I know everything she has endured, and you will pay for that, too. But first, you will tell me where you have hidden her mother, or I will make Hasan's fate seem like a paradise filled with houris."

The Sultan paled. "I do not know!"

"Tell me!"

"I do not know!" the Sultan shouted. "Much like you, I could not bear to look upon her. The enchantress who bound her took Briska into her service."

"Where?"

"Somewhere far to the north, where it is cold and snow falls from the skies, or so she said. But that was years ago! She could be anywhere now!"

An enchantress powerful enough to hide Briska from him? Not possible.

"Who is this enchantress?" Amani demanded.

"Mistress Kun, the courtesan."

Amani burst out laughing. "The contortionist, you mean? Your left testicle has more magic than Mistress Kun. Why, every man at court has had her, one way or another. Tell me the truth, old man, or I'll set your hairy balls on fire."

The Sultan glowered. "The woman may be free with her affections, but her magic was powerful enough to bind you, and Briska. Who do you think enslaved you to that tarnished lamp?"

Common gossip in court had held that her youthful appearance and sexual prowess were through magical means, but then, most of the court considered owls and broken mirrors bad luck, too. They were a superstitious lot.

"If this is true, then she may have more to answer for than you do." Including how a lowly courtesan had managed to hide her powers from him, Amani thought but didn't say. "Tell me where she is and I will let you live."

"I don't know that, either. She left my court some time ago. Maram may know, for she trained with her, but I do not." The Sultan threw his arms up to shield himself. "Don't hurt me! I am telling you everything I know!"

Which wasn't much, but it was something,

at least. Amani narrowed his eyes. "Divorce her, and I will let you live."

"I already have. Before she was bound as a djinn. Because it is not fitting for a sultan to be married to a slave." The Sultan sniffed.

"And what of her dowry?" Amani asked.

"Slaves cannot own property. I have it still."

And he'd profited mightily from it, Amani didn't doubt. He lifted his chin. "See that you have it ready for her when I return. For I shall free her, and when I do, she will return to claim what is hers. Down to the smallest copper coin." He'd endured two decades of slavery because this man refused to divorce a wife who did not love him. A little payback was called for. "And if you think to withhold any of it, I will make sure you die an agonising death. After I tell Princess Maram's husband everything about her past." Not that there was much Aladdin did not know, but the Sultan wouldn't know that. He still believed Aladdin was a prince, after all.

The Sultan paled. "None of this is Maram's fault. Leave her out of it."

Amani grinned. "That's up to you, old man."

He cast a portal, and departed.

Twenty-Nine

When he'd finished an evening meal lifted from the Sultan's kitchens on his way out of the palace, Amani sat in his own hall and attempted another search spell.

He sent the spell north, questing wherever he found snow, not for the courtesan, but for Briska. But no matter how hard he looked, still he could not find her.

So he turned his attention to the courtesan, Mistress Kun. A woman who'd managed to hide her magic from him, keep him from finding Briska and, the biggest insult of all, she'd bound him to that brass lamp.

He paced the length of his hall and back again, sensing the spell seeking through the northern snow for the courtesan. It should not take so long. Why, he'd never taken more than a moment to find anyone, no matter where in the world they were. To take so long…to fail twice! Why, it was unheard of. Had his enslavement dulled his powers, perhaps?

Amani broke off the search and stormed outside. From the courtyard, he could see the dry riverbed from which his castle drew its water in the wintertime. Winter was a while off yet, but there were autumn storms brewing in the Middle Sea that would suit his purposes perfectly. Finding a storm was harder than finding a person – if he could not even fill the water tanks at home, then his time tied to the lamp truly had weakened him.

His magic slowed as it hit a patch of moist air, closer than he'd expected. Amani took a deep breath. Now all he had to do was summon a strong enough breeze to blow it over to that low pressure system and keep them together long enough for the storm to make landfall here instead of one of the countries further north.

Holding the storm system together took most of his focus, and what he had left he pushed into steering the behemoth to where he wanted it. For hours, he battled the beast, or perhaps it was only moments – Amani did not know. But as the storm hit the wall of heat rising from the desert sands, Amani knew he had succeeded. He eased back from the roiling mass of clouds, content to watch nature take its course as the clouds dropped their deluge before fleeing over the mountains in defeat.

Rain filled the streams, turning every depression into a rivulet, tumbling headlong toward the river. Amani felt the water like blood rushing through his veins, spreading its cold fingers across the land. The desert bloomed and all manner of beasts surfaced from the sand to slake their thirst.

But still Amani waited, for the flood had not yet reached his home.

The river began to run, a trickle at first, before it became a steady stream. A distant roar heralded the rushing surge that swept all before it. Waves licked hungrily at the high walls of his castle, but the magic-reinforced stone kept it at bay. He waited for the first wash to take the silt and debris out to sea before he opened the aqueducts, allowing the cleaner water to flow through the pipework into his holding tanks.

When he brought Briska here, to his home, she would have a better bathhouse than her daughter's. All he had to do was find her, or the courtesan who had stolen her away.

No common courtesan would keep him from the woman he loved, Amani swore, as he sent out another searching spell, secure in the knowledge that his powers were stronger than ever.

Thirty

Amani stood on the road outside Maram's gates, wishing he did not have to be here. But he dared not portal into her home without an invitation, especially not when he intended to be even deeper in her debt before the day was out.

A debt he would make that worthless courtesan pay, when he had her in his grasp.

Amani had taken the time to bathe and dress appropriately for visiting a prince, as that's what everyone believed Aladdin to be, and Amani had no intention of changing that.

He'd worked too hard to build Aladdin's reputation as a prince to destroy it now.

The guards stopped him at the gate, but politely, as befit someone of his stature. "Your name and your business, master, so that we may announce your arrival to the prince."

"I am the sorcerer, Lord Amani, and I wish to congratulate the prince and his new bride on their nuptials," Amani said smoothly. Now she was married, he could not visit Maram without her husband present. Never mind that she was an ex-courtesan and he'd lived alone with her for weeks without any impropriety…as though he'd do any such thing with Briska's daughter!

One of the guards headed into the house, before returning to escort Amani inside.

Maram rose to welcome him into her sitting room, where he'd spent many pleasant hours conversing with her while they were trapped on the savannah, but Aladdin stood by the wall, looking as awkward as ever in such fine surroundings. A good man and a merchant's son, but no prince. And yet, of all the masters Amani had been forced to serve, Aladdin was the only one he was willing to share a cup of wine with, without poisoning the contents.

Aladdin ducked his head in a brief bow. "It is lovely to see you again so soon, Lord Amani. Forgive me, but I am on my way to see my mother, who I hope to persuade to take up residence here, at Maram's request. I'm sure my wife will entertain you in my absence." He moved to depart.

"You're leaving us alone?" Amani blurted out. Did the boy not know what this would do to his wife's reputation?

"We both know this palace belongs to Maram, and she is well able to entertain any visitor she pleases in her home," Aladdin said with a smile. He rubbed his thumb across a ring on his finger in a gesture that seemed completely unconscious, but Amani knew better, for he recognised the ring. The weak djinn who was bound to it was no match for Amani in most things, but his combination of invisibility and unusual physical strength still made him a formidable protector for Princess Maram. And an unseen chaperone, who would tell Aladdin everything that had passed between them in Aladdin's absence.

Maram sighed. "He has no idea. I've never met a man who cared less for his reputation. Amani, if you'd be kind enough to help him travel to his mother's unseen…"

Amani opened a portal, and gestured for Aladdin to enter. Aladdin departed, and Amani waited for the portal to close completely before he said, "He might be gone, but it was not my intention to keep any part of our discussion a secret from your husband. Perhaps another time…" He gritted his teeth. He didn't want to come back. He needed her help now.

"I keep no secrets from Aladdin, but there are some things I think he does not wish to know," Maram said softly. "Like how to free djinn, for example." She beckoned a servant forward and accepted a cloth-wrapped parcel from the girl. Maram then held it out to Amani. "I had the lamp polished. It's not gold, but…I thought you might like to keep it. And…inside it, you will find something that may help you in your quest. Something…you will need, but that your pride will not allow you to ask for. There are other ways to free djinn, but they require several sorcerers working in cooperation and the results can be unpredictable. This way is better."

Amani swallowed, then held his breath as he unwrapped the lamp and forced himself to lift the lid. The lamp was stuffed with what appeared to be a roll of fine linen, but inside the linen was a glass vial of some dark liquid. He held it up to the light, and his gut clenched as the liquid glowed red.

"I cannot accept this." The words burst from him unbidden. This was royal blood, the same as that which ran in her father's veins and her own. With this, he could curse the Sultan's entire bloodline.

"Then why did you come, if not for more of my blood to free her?" Maram's dark eyes, so much like her mother's, were wide with curiosity.

"I cannot find her," he confessed. "She is a djinn, bound to serve whatever master holds her in thrall, just as I was. And she serves Mistress Kun, who I cannot find, either."

Maram drew in a sharp breath. "Kun? The

courtesan? No, she can only cast seduction magic, like me. The occasional small blessing or curse, like she did for Vardan. She couldn't possibly be powerful enough to hide from you. Why, Mother always said you were the most powerful sorcerer in the world!"

Amani grunted. "I am, or I was. But there are some forms of magic I cannot perform, and cloaking, invisibility, is one of them. And she has done something that hides herself and your mother from me. Please…is there anything she said, in passing, perhaps, that might help me locate her, and maybe your mother, too?"

Maram spread her arms wide. "She is a courtesan, the kind who travels for both business and pleasure. She could be anywhere in the world. The last place I saw her was Beacon Isle, before I met my husband. But if you wish to get a message to her…there is a city on a swamp, a republic, like the one in the ancient legends, with a port that is a favourite among crusaders. She keeps a palace on one of the islands in the floating city."

"She's from a floating crusader city?" Even

Amani didn't believe it.

Maram smiled faintly. "No, she has a house there, is all. She was born in the Kunlun Mountains, far to the east, where the horse people war with the middle kingdom, and no one truly wins, or so she says. There are magical peach trees in the mountains where she was born, so powerful that one bite of the fruit can grant you immortality, or so it is said. What I do know is that I have known her for most of my life, and she has not aged a day. Perhaps immortality is possible, after all. The floating city…while I have not been there myself, I have heard many crusaders speak of it. It is no myth."

"I have heard she is in the far north, where it snows."

"Perhaps. Who can say? I last saw her at Beacon Isle, in the northern seas. There are tales of places further north where the ground is made of ice, ice that never melts." Maram laid a hand on Amani's wrist. "I do not know where Mistress Kun is, but if I were to go searching for her, I would go first to the floating palace and leave a message, telling her you wish to find her. For me. And you will take the lamp and the vial, because I ask only one thing of you: that you find my mother, free her, and bring her home to me."

"Princess…"

Maram clasped her hands before her. "If the most powerful sorcerer in the world cannot find her, then I fear she is lost forever. Please, Amani. If you love her…if you ever loved her…"

Amani dropped to one knee. "I have never loved any woman as I love Briska, and I will never love another. I will find her, and I shall free her, and I shall bring her here to show her the wonderful woman her daughter has become. This I swear."

"Ah, men and their oaths. Actions speak louder than words, Amani. Go find her!"

He rose, bowed, and left, with the lamp tucked firmly under his arm.

Thirty-One

Amani stayed in the floating city long enough to determine that it was indeed real, and built on poles thrust deep into the swamp. It smelled like the river at the end of the spring, too, when the water dried up and formed shallow, stagnant ponds that would make a man so sick he'd die if he drank from them.

Kun the courtesan kept a house there, and Amani left a message with her servants, but they had no idea when she might return. He gathered it had been some time since they'd seen their mistress, and Amani didn't blame her. He never stayed home when it smelled like the river had died. Instead, he'd travelled during that part of the year, including the summer he'd paid a visit to the Sultan's court and first glimpsed Briska. The woman had mesmerised him with her eyes alone. Almost like magic, and yet it was not.

Once he left the city, though, he found himself with two choices. Either he could follow the silk road east, or the crusaders' way north. He cared little for silk and less for horse people, whatever those might be, but he was curious to see what had inspired the religious zealots in their crusade, so he headed north, as it had been some time since he'd last seen snow.

But every city he stopped at…no one had ever heard of a courtesan named Kun. The more prosperous cities had heard of Princess Maram, though, and they sang her praises. When he mentioned he was on a quest for her, doors opened as they never had before. A powerful sorcerer they looked upon with suspicion, but Princess Maram's envoy was beyond reproach.

By the time he reached the ports along the northern sea, Amani had all but given up asking for Kun. It was as though the woman had never existed, which he knew couldn't be true.

Weary beyond belief, he took a room in an inn in Kasmirus that had an enormous skull mounted above a sign that proclaimed it was the Dragon's Head, for some famous dragonslayer had once slept there. And left the beast's head behind.

He claimed a table near the roaring fire in the crowded taproom, for the winter in those parts was biting cold at the best of times. He refused the ale and asked for some wine, but these northern barbarians had never heard of grapes, so their wine tasted more of raw spirit than the fruit it was brewed from. Perhaps they needed the liquid warmth, with the air so cold. He sipped it slowly, letting the stuff warm all the way down to his toes before calling for another.

A black-haired barmaid brought it, dumping his drink on the table before sitting across from him, unasked.

Amani waved her away. "I'm in no need of company tonight. Better sell your affections elsewhere."

She raised her head and met his eyes as she took a deep draught from his cup. "A slave cannot afford such things, anyway."

He laughed. "Your mind must be addled! Me, a slave? Take care, girl, for I am a lord with a castle back home."

"You are a slave, because I bound you, and only I can break the bond between you and the lamp. Who do you serve?" she demanded.

Amani met her gaze squarely. "Most times, I serve myself, but right now, I have the honour of doing a small favour for Princess Maram."

Surprise flickered in her eyes for a moment, so quickly Amani might have imagined it, but he knew he had not.

"What message do you bring from Her Highness?" she asked.

Amani took a careful sip of his drink, wiped his mouth, then said, "Not so much a message as a request. She wants to see her mother."

Mistress Kun smiled, for the girl could be no one else, though she looked a decade younger than Amani remembered her. "And she sent you. She always was a clever girl. Because no one wants to find Briska more than you do. Did her father give her the lamp, or did she find it on her own? Ah, it does not matter, not truly. The real question is: what are you willing to offer me for the information you want?"

For Briska? "Anything," Amani answered.

Thirty-Two

And that's how he'd ended up back in the desert, where this whole mess started. Well, perhaps not quite the same place, for Briska's bed was cold and empty, but now he stood at the blocked-off entrance to an underground city. A city with no people inside and, he discovered as he used magic to shift the enormous entrance stone, stale air that said no one had been there for some time.

For a moment, he feared that the treasure he sought would be long gone, but the glitter of gold beside the entrance caught his eye.

Several statues were lined up along the wall, all life-sized. If anyone intended to steal something, these would be the first items he'd take, yet here they were, untouched.

With increasing hope in his step, Amani headed into the tunnel.

As he'd moved away from the city gates, the air had grown fresher, fed by the ventilation shafts in the ceiling that ran deep into the earth, but the dust on the ground had also become deeper, muffling his footsteps. A closer look revealed it was fine sand and not dust, undoubtedly carried down the air shafts by the swirling sandstorms outside.

Aside from the dust, the place had been left in a surprisingly orderly state, as though the city residents intended to return, but had been prevented from doing so. Bad air hadn't driven them out, the usual culprit in underground places, and the place hadn't been sacked, so…what else could it be?

He approached one of the numerous wells around the city, and peered in. He should have been greeted by the drip and rush of the underground aquifer, but all he heard was silence. Amani bit his lip and sent his magic questing after the water.

The well was dry, and so was the next, though the cavern where the water should have been was deep enough to hold more water than a city of this size could ever need. He followed the twisting cavern, carved by the ancient, underground river, until he found the natural stone dam that had once kept the enormous reservoir secure beneath the city. No more – the rock was cracked all the way across, and the water had followed its natural course, down to a natural depression where it leaped to the surface in a bubbling spring. A spring so new there were no trees around it yet, though a clump of tiny date palms huddled together in solidarity, proclaiming their intention of claiming this waterhole as their own.

He knew the waterhole – it was Philemon's folly. Which made this city…Tasnim. A city guarded by the djinn who served Aladdin. A djinn who had no liking for Amani.

Amani swore softly. If Kun had intended to humiliate him, she'd chosen her quest well. His lamp prison had been stored in the treasure rooms here for a time, at the command of another, younger and comelier enchantress than Kun. If Philemon had owned an enchanted object that negated all magic in its vicinity, rendering an enchanter like himself powerless, it would be in his deepest treasury, where Amani's lamp had been. For what better way to protect his other priceless treasures than with a powerful magic object?

After an hour of walking and still he hadn't reached the bottom of the tunnels, Amani waved his magical light source to a halt and summoned a waterskin to quench his thirst, for there was no other drinkable water in the city.

Finally, he arrived at the city's treasury, and a stone door heavier than the rest stood in his way. He used magic to shift it aside, then sent his magical ball of light inside first, as a matter of caution. If a magic-nullifying artefact lay inside, he would rather lose his light source than all of his powers at once.

Yet the light glowed serenely as it bobbed across the room, so Amani followed it. There was less dust on the floor here — fewer air shafts, most likely — but there were gold coins strewn around, as though someone had tried to take some with them and not cared if they dropped a few.

The scattered coins grew more numerous, the deeper he ventured into the treasury, until he reached a sort of altar, with an open chest before it. Whatever had once graced the altar was now gone, leaving only a circle in the dust to show it had ever existed.

Amani was willing to wager that whatever had sat there was the item he wanted. Without it, Kun would never tell him where to find Briska.

Then again, she hadn't known what it looked like, just what effect it had.

Amani took a moment to contemplate his options. Perhaps he could provide the courtesan with a magic dampening device after all.

Thirty-Three

Right. This time, he thought he had it.

Amani set the lamp down in the sand, then backed up against the outer wall, as far as he could get away from it while still in his castle compound.

If this worked, he could meet Kun before nightfall, and have Briska in his arms before morning.

If it didn't…

He sighed. If it didn't, then he would have to seek out some even more ancient scrolls in the hope that he'd find the spell he needed, for he'd scoured through every spell he had.

Amani took a deep breath, and bit his lip. A flame-trail flickered across the sand, headed for the lamp. It touched the wick, and the lamp flared to life, flames dancing a little in the breeze. At almost the same moment, the trail extinguished itself, leaving nothing but wispy smoke and a line of scorched sand to mark its passage.

So far, so good.

Amani conjured a ball of light, like the one he'd used to light his way in Tasnim. He lobbed the ball at the lamp.

The ball arced up, reaching the peak of its flight, before it began to fall. Then it winked out. Gone.

Amani measured the distance with his eyes. That had to be…twenty feet, at least. Hard to tell at that height.

He conjured another ball and sent it skimming along the sand. It vanished sooner than he expected. Not twenty feet at all – more like thirty.

So the spell had a radius thirty feet wide…but did it stretch up thirty feet, too?

Amani used magic to scoop up some sand, then floated it to a point fifty feet above the lamp. Then, he let it sink, foot by foot, until it was just above thirty feet. So far, so good.

Another foot. Fine. Another. A third…

The sand dropped, and no spell he cast at it could touch it. He was powerless to do anything but watch as the sand buried the lamp, extinguishing it.

He sent a magical breeze toward the lamp to blow the sand away. It took some concentration to ensure he'd scoured away all the sand, leaving the lamp as shiny as it had looked when Maram handed it to him.

It looked nothing like the tarnished piece of trash it had been when he'd been trapped in it. If Amani himself scarcely recognised his prison, Kun would surely not know the difference. As long as it negated all magic within thirty feet of it, she would not care what it was.

He squinted at the sun. It was perhaps not too late to portal to the northern town where Kun had insisted they meet once he'd found what she wanted.

Just the thought of having Briska in his arms again…tonight, even…

Amani opened a portal, pausing only to conjure warm clothes for himself as he stepped from desert sands to deep snow.

Thirty-Four

Kasmirus was a tropical paradise compared to this place, Amani fumed as he tried to move closer to the fire without actually sitting in the flames. This inn's fire was larger than the one in the Dragon's Head, but the very air seemed to drink the warmth from it before it reached him. He'd downed two drinks, enough to stop him from shivering, but it did little to slow the creeping numbness in his fingers and toes. If Kun didn't turn up soon, he'd head home and return on the morrow. He had no intention of trying to sleep in this frozen nightmare of a place.

He signalled to the innkeeper for another drink. If Kun had not arrived by the time Amani had drained his cup, he would depart.

A cloaked figure came into the taproom, almost bent double under the weight of snow on her cloak. And it was a woman, so ancient-looking Amani wondered how she could still be alive. The innkeeper took her cloak with reverence, and the taproom fell silent.

Beneath her cloak, the crone wore a gown that was more suitable for the desert than a blizzard, yet she did not seem to feel the cold. She made her laborious way across the room to Amani's table. The nearest place to the fire.

He debated whether to offer his seat to the old woman, but she made up her mind before he did. She perched on the bench across from him and patted the table, indicating for the innkeeper to set her drink down.

Amani rose, then bowed. "I must beg your forgiveness, revered grandmother, but I am waiting for someone. I will move to another table."

"And what makes you think I'll let you?"

The crone lifted her head, and Amani found himself staring into Kun's unwrinkled eyes. She pressed a finger to her lips. "I hope you brought what I asked for. If you've dragged me out into a blizzard to beg and make excuses, I will turn you into one of those squirrel things so prized for their fur hereabouts. Vair, I think they are called."

Amani had no idea what a squirrel was, but he did know he didn't wish to become one. "Mistress Kun." He ducked his head and returned to his seat. "I believe I've found the object you wanted."

He pulled the lamp from the pouch at his waist and set it on the table.

Kun squinted at it, then tapped it. "It looks like an ordinary lamp. Aren't you sleeping in its twin these days?" She cackled with laughter, sounding like a crone.

"I will not rest until I have found Briska," Amani snapped.

Kun grinned. "Is the compulsion to obey getting painful for you? So much for being a powerful sorcerer, when you're rendered useless by a little headache." She lowered her voice to a whisper. "And it will only get worse. If this isn't what I asked for, you will fail in your quest."

So she knew about the skull-splitting headaches djinn suffered when they resisted their masters. A malady he would suffer from no more, though she did not know that.

"You asked for a magical object that can dampen any magic around it. This lamp does precisely that – at a radius of thirty feet," Amani said.

Kun snorted. "Do I look like a fool to you? If this was anything more than a common lamp, you would see me as I truly am. None of this white hair." She waved her hand at the white tresses that crowned her youthful face.

"It needs to be lit," Amani said, conjuring a handful of flames. He held the flames to the lamp wick until the oil caught.

Kun gasped.

So did Amani.

Before him sat a teenage girl, wearing a short tunic so thin it was almost transparent, leaving none of her skeletal body to the imagination. The only ornament she still wore was a ring that sat loosely on her finger, giving off a red light that shimmered across her skin, as though setting the very blood in her veins aglow. Magic of some kind, he guessed.

"And I thought all those muscles were an illusion. No wonder you seduced the queen so easily," the girl snapped. Her eyes betrayed her – they belonged to no child. "You should show your true form to young Maram. She will keep you close to home, no tiresome quests, and make you serve her in the bedchamber instead. She is a gifted courtesan, as capable of giving pleasure as she is at receiving it. You will come to enjoy it, I am sure."

The very thought of lying with Maram – Briska's daughter, no less! – disgusted Amani, and he made no attempt to hide it.

"Enough," he said. "You have what you asked for. Now, tell me where she is."

Kun wagged an admonishing finger at him. "Oh no. You have not told me how to control this thing yet."

"When the lamp is lit, the spell is active. When you extinguish the flame..." Amani dipped his fingers in his drink, then used the dripping digits to pinch the wick out. "When the light is out, magic may be used again." He waved his hand and his torso was once again covered by a thick fur vest.

In the blink of an eye, Kun had changed, too. The poor peasant girl was gone, replaced by the curvy courtesan he'd once bedded. She pursed her lips, as if to beg for a kiss. "You must think me a fool, Amani. This is not the treasure I asked for, but a poor imitation you have conjured to trick me. Does the disgraced queen mean so little to you, that you won't even go on a simple quest to save her?"

"I would do anything for her!" Amani protested.

A wide, predatory smile showed too much of Kun's perfect teeth. "Pledge yourself to me. Become my bed slave, and when I decide you have atoned for trying to trick me, perhaps I will tell you where to find the woman. If you still want her, once you have had me." She fluttered her eyelashes. Once, long ago, the slight movement had fanned his desire into a raging blaze. Now, he could only see the starving child who'd been seated across from him only moments before.

"No. You have what you asked for, I swear it. Now tell me where she is!" Amani roared, rising to his feet.

People were staring, but Kun paid them no heed. She was a crone once more, even more frail-looking than before. She raised her hand to wave, the ring on her finger seeming to glow red in the firelight. "Farewell, sorcerer, and good luck finding your snow queen without my help. When you are ready to offer me what I want, then I will help you."

She marched across the room, pausing only to pull on her cloak, before sweeping out of the door into the whirling snow.

Amani swore, then called for another drink. He'd need it if he intended to go outside into the snow to cast a portal home. At least he still had…

He stared at the table, but the lamp was gone.

The bitch had distracted him, somehow, and stolen it, taking with her his only chance of finding Briska.

The innkeeper brought his drink. Amani

drained it, then ordered another. He may as well drink himself senseless, for he was the biggest fool the world had ever seen. And poor Briska would pay the price for his stupidity, once again.

He deserved to lose her.

Thirty-Five

"How fares Zuleika, and her prince?"

Briska blinked. Kun's face filled the mirror, and she'd asked a question. Haltingly, Briska begged her to repeat it.

When she had, Briska answered, "As well as to be expected. She is warming to him, and I think it will only be a matter of time before they give in to their mutual attraction."

"Good, good. You have done well. I have a reward for you."

This was unusual. "Thank you?" Briska ventured.

Kun continued, "You asked for my protection from magic while you are here in your citadel. At great personal cost, I have procured such a spell for you. Here." She held out a brass lamp, and Briska hurried to take it from her.

It wasn't until Briska's fingers touched the glass that she realised how silly she'd been. Spells passed through the mirror, but a solid object could not, surely. Yet her hands closed around metal, and she now held the lamp in her hands, while Kun's were empty.

"Once lit, the lamp will extinguish all magic around it. But when the lamp goes out, your protection goes with it, and you must light it again." Kun peered into the mirror. "If you place is within ten yards of the entrance to your palace, no one will be able to bring magic inside or cast a spell anywhere near you."

"But only when it is lit," Briska corrected. "Right now, it does nothing." She stared back at Kun. "I'd best keep it away from the mirror, then, for if the lamp removes magic, it will surely turn this back into an ordinary mirror."

Kun laughed. "I doubt it. The magic

enchanting that mirror is more powerful than any living spellcaster could produce. The little lamp will not harm the mirror, or its magic. But the mirror is more than ten yards from your gates, so if you place the lamp at the entrance, you will have nothing to worry about."

"Yes, Mistress." The words that came out of Briska's mouth were the last thing she wanted to say. She had plenty to worry about, not least of which was this new, strange artefact that Kun was only giving her now. Did that mean the current couple she was trying to matchmake would attack her, and it would be worse than Hansel, Gretel, Gerda and Kai combined?

But two decades of servitude had resigned Briska to her fate. Amani was dead and gone, and Maram was surely happy with her devoted lover. Briska's ex-husband surely had plenty of other wives and concubines and perhaps even a new queen to keep him amused. Anyone who knew her had surely forgotten her by now. Except Kun, who never failed to bring another assignment, a new couple to match.

Briska had given up any hope of freedom, for the more successful she was, the more couples Kun gave her.

Nevertheless, she thanked Kun again before the woman disappeared from the mirror, and Briska returned to the delicate task of transforming a warming friendship into something more. If only the girl would forget the incident with the man's brother...

Thirty-Six

"Another!" Amani slurred, waving his hand aimlessly. He couldn't recall how many of these potent jugs of wine he'd drunk, but as long as he could still think, he would drink. For wine was harder and harder to get in his homeland, with that new religion that said you shouldn't drink the stuff.

"How much more do you think you'll need, friend?" the innkeeper asked. He spread his arms. "The taproom is closed, and everyone else has gone to bed. I will go soon, too, and I would advise you to do the same."

"There is only one bed I want, and it belongs to the queen in her snowy citadel," Amani announced. "But I will never find her, so I must drink to forget. More wine!"

The innkeeper sighed. "Her bed is cold as ice, my friend, and best forgotten." He set a second cup on the table, then filled first Amani's and then its companion. He lifted his cup in a toast. "To forgetting."

Amani raised his cup in salute, then downed the contents, ready to bring oblivion.

Thirty-Seven

Briska didn't take her eyes off the pair. She'd matched enough couples to know this was the crucial night. She was no seer, so she didn't know the precise moment, but they were both humming with so much…potential for love, something important would happen tonight, and she would ensure it was the right something.

She watched them eat without even a twinge of hunger, unable to remember how long it had been since she'd last eaten. Years, maybe.

He asked the girl to dance, then stood up

with her, to Briska's surprise. Oh, commoners sometimes danced with the opposite sex, but nobility like this pair were not unlike her people – the ladies danced together, and the men just watched.

Ah, it surprised Zuleika, too – but it made her smile, so that was all right. And it gave the pair an excuse to link hands, which certainly helped. The room raged with lust – the townspeople might be invisible to anyone else, but Briska saw them clearly. The musicians caught the mood and changed the tune, so that the dancers broke from their long chain into pairs.

Vardan's spirits soared as he took the enchantress in his arms. He needed no help from Briska at all, for his feelings for Zuleika had proceeded far beyond lust.

But nothing more could happen in this crowded room. Vardan was the ruler of these people, and while he was certain of his own feelings, he was unsure of hers. A ruler would not want to lose face before his people.

Briska blinked. No, it wasn't about losing face at all. He cared what his people thought about her, if she rejected him. How strange. A ruler loved by his people.

So the push must come from Zuleika, not Vardan.

Zuleika's tongue darted out, moistening her lips, and it gave Briska an idea.

She concentrated, intensifying the girl's thirst just as one of the servants brought a tray of drinks into the hall. There. She had the pair close to the door, and if they chatted for long enough, one of them would…yes!

Vardan took her hand and led her out.

Briska leaned forward, so her nose almost touched the glass, as she watched them go to…a library? A peculiar place for a tryst, but there was no accounting for some people's taste.

Sure enough, this pair were soon distracted by a hand mirror, their lust fading fast.

Not if Briska had any say in the matter, she resolved grimly, hitting them both with a seduction spell. "Resist that, I dare you," she muttered.

She gave them ten seconds, but it only took them six before they kissed. Briska knew her job well. She allowed herself a silent victory cheer.

A scream pierced the silence, so loud it shook an icicle free from the ceiling to crash into the floor behind Briska.

Briska cursed. What had she done this time?

Had Zuleika heard her? Seen her? Somehow known Briska was there?

All colour drained from Briska's face. If she knew this was Briska's second mistake…if she could pin the blame for Thorn on her…

Briska watched with mounting dread as she saw Zuleika flee from the other brother, knowing her flight would end in her casting a portal to take her far away. Far from Beacon Isle, but to where?

Here. Where Briska was no match for the powerful young enchantress.

Briska fell to her knees. She was doomed. The enchantress would destroy her, and rightly so.

Briska's eyes fell on the lamp. Kun's mysterious gift.

She could scarcely conjure a spark any more, so it took some time with the tinder box before a trembling flame sat atop the lamp wick.

Briska breathed a sigh of relief. She was safe, for no magic could touch her here, and the girl's portal would never reach this eyrie.

Thirty-Eight

"Sleeping on tables is not a wise thing to do. What was Kai thinking? My fool of a husband should have offered you a bed," a woman grumbled, far too loud for Amani's liking.

He lifted his head from his distinctly uncomfortable pillow, glad for the dimness of the taproom. "I was not sleeping. I was merely resting my pounding head for a moment," Amani announced. He reached into his pocket, plucked out a coin and tossed it on the table. "For some quiet while I rest it a little more."

She laughed. "You'll get no quiet here. Last

night's blizzard has blown itself out, and as soon as the old men of the village have nagged their sons into shovelling a path, they will be gossiping about whatever war they fought in that everyone else has forgotten, it was so long ago."

"I need to find the queen. In her icy castle…and her icy bed." So much for forgetting. He hadn't drunk enough, after all. "No. What I need is more wine."

"What you need is breakfast and some water, for you are not right in the head. The Snow Queen has been dead these fifteen years and more."

Amani shook his head. "No, that can't be possible. She lives, I am certain of it." Maram wouldn't have lied. Not to him. Djinn couldn't die.

The innkeeper's wife folded her arms across her chest. "I stabbed the bitch myself. She kidnapped Kai, and nearly killed him."

Briska? Kidnap some innkeeper? Why?

But Amani knew the answer. He'd been a slave himself, forced to obey every stupid order he was given. She'd done it because someone had ordered her to.

"Even if she'd somehow survived being stabbed in the heart, she'd still need to eat. And no one's seen her come down from her mountain since the day she kidnapped Kai," the woman said firmly. "She's dead and she deserved it."

Punishing a slave for her master's crimes? Despicable. If this woman had truly tried to kill Briska, then Briska deserved justice. But first he had to find her.

"Which mountain? Where?" he demanded.

She narrowed her eyes. "You're a bigger fool than my husband, if you plan to go up there in winter. You'll die for certain, for no one will venture up the mountain until the snow melts in spring."

Amani seized her shoulders. "Tell me, and I will let you live." He should not be offering this woman her life, not when it was already forfeit for her attempt to murder Briska. Then again, he was no king or lawmaker, and meting out justice was not his job.

She thrust out a hand and pointed. "Step through the door and you'll see it. Look for the frozen waterfall, and it's perched on the crags above it. Impossible to reach, even in summer, unless you have a witch to help you. If you go up there, the shepherds will bring your body back for burial come spring." Tears formed in her eyes. "If she had not taken Kai, I would not have gone up there. As it was…we almost didn't make it back. My family would have mourned us both. If you go up there, think of the family who will come here searching for you. Who will die on the mountain for you?"

Amani released her. "No one will die for me. I have no family left. She is all the family I ever wanted, and…" He blinked, forcing back what could only be tears. He would not cry in front of this strange, violent woman. "I must go after her, for she is all I have left."

"Wait until spring. Maybe I could show you the path I took…"

Amani shook his head. "She has waited long enough. So have I." He rounded the table and headed for the door.

Without even a backward glance toward the innkeeper's wife, Amani headed out into the snow. His breath froze in his throat, but he strode on, not even pausing as he conjured one layer of fur and then another over his winter clothes. When he reached the outskirts of the village and could be certain there was no one watching, he cast a portal to take him to the top of the glittering waterfall. Mere ice and stone would not keep him from Briska. Not now he was so close.

Thirty-Nine

Amani landed in snow, tumbling head over heels in a headlong flight he could not seem to stop until he hit something that knocked the breath from his lungs. If the snow hadn't been so deep, the fall would have killed him. As it was…he winced as he felt what had to be one, maybe even two cracked ribs.

He rose painfully to his feet, scanning the snow for something, anything. His portal, or the icy spires he'd glimpsed from the valley, but he saw neither. In a world of moonlit white beneath a still dark predawn sky, at least there was sound. His boots crunched through the snow, as the wind whistled off the rocks. And there was a dull roaring sound, just at the edge of hearing.

The waterfall!

Just like the floodwaters filling the river outside his castle, only vertical instead of horizontal.

He followed the sound of water, wishing with all his might that it would lead him to Briska. If he didn't find her here, he didn't know what he'd do. Where else he could search. How did you find one woman in a whole world of people? A woman who couldn't be found by magical means…

Amani's head spun, as though he'd run too fast, but he couldn't seem to catch his breath. The aftereffects of wine had never made him feel like this before.

And cold! Where had his furs gone? And his shirt? He must have lost them in the snow somewhere. At least his ribs hurt less in the cold. There was that, he told himself, as he trudged on, wrapping his arms around himself in a fruitless attempt to keep warm. He tried to conjure a cloak, a blanket, anything to keep him warm, but whatever had stolen his breath had stolen his magic, too.

What in all that was holy could do such a thing? If it was Kun, he would kill her. No magic necessary. He'd wrap his hands around her throat and squeeze until she stopped breathing. Nothing would get between him and Briska ever again.

Amani blinked. Was that…glass? He dragged his numb feet up to the wall and pressed his hand to it. No, not glass. Ice, stealing his remaining body heat as he tried and failed to pull his palm from the wall. Then he managed to get his other hand stuck, and Amani knew he was in trouble.

His whole body was numb. Death would come to claim him soon. At least he would meet his fate standing, for he could not lie down in the snow with both hands stuck to a wall.

He waited for the memories to come, the last thing he would ever see, to distract him as he passed into the next world.

As if on command, the best came first.

Briska walked into view, as perfect as the first time he'd seen her. A marble statue come to life.

Yet this wasn't a memory. It couldn't be. For there it was.

Nestled in her hands was a lamp. His lamp.

Forty

Briska stared at the flickering flame, wondering if something so tiny could truly protect her from the enchantress. She didn't dare look in the mirror again, just in case the girl saw her.

It took her a long moment to remember all of Kun's instructions about the lamp. Not only did she need to light it, but it had a limited range — in order to stop anyone from entering the palace, the lamp needed to be near the gates.

Her heart froze in her chest. What if her forgetfulness had allowed someone to enter the palace already? Even now, the girl could be inside, creeping up on her.

Briska cradled the lamp in her hands, holding it close to her chest as she took it to the entrance hall. She hunched her shoulders over it, hating the feeling that she was being watched.

She set the lamp in the middle of the entrance hall, where it looked as out of place as a child's discarded shoe.

While she'd been distracted, the sky had begun to lighten, building up to dawn, and now she could see the valley spread out before her, through the thin, transparent walls. A view she rarely looked at any more, for what was there to look at when everything was covered with snow? Even the waterfall was frozen.

She fancied she heard someone say her name, but a quick glance at the gates told her there was no one out there.

In here, then, she thought with a shiver. Briska edged closer to the lamp, until her boots almost touched it. She turned slowly in a circle, scanning the room with all her normal senses. Even if the enchantress was invisible, she still had to breathe.

Twice she circled, and still she did not find the girl. But there were marks on the wall, marring her view of the waterfall. Briska stepped closer to investigate.

Why, they looked like handprints, two of them, and a thin trail of blood frozen to the wall leading down. Quite macabre, really. If the girl thought to frighten her…

Briska held her hand up to the print. No woman had made these. A large man, maybe, or a bear might have. But white bears did not climb so high, away from the sea and their source of sustenance.

Whoever had left them wouldn't have survived long up here. But she would have to go outside and clean them off, or stare at them every time she looked to the waterfall.

She opened the gates and stepped out, careful to keep to the path that now lay buried under a layer of ice and snow. One wrong step would bury her for good – or at least until Kun came looking for her.

Snow had piled up beneath the handprints, perfectly placed for her to stand on so she could reach the marks. Ugh, the blood was worse than she'd thought, smeared down the wall in two wide, pink streaks. Briska set one boot on the drift, testing her footing before putting all her weight on it.

The drift groaned, not unlike a bear.

Briska backed away, darting a glance behind her to make sure the gate wasn't too far away. Once she rounded the corner of the palace, she'd run. Before the bear could rise.

It groaned again, and flung out a paw. No, not a paw. A bloody hand, tinted blue. It was a man in the snowdrift, and if she didn't do something, he'd be a dead man.

Taking a deep breath, Briska forced herself back the way she'd come. She thrust her gloved hands into the snow and grasped the man's shoulder. Brushing away the snow, she found his head, and used all her strength to roll him over, so she could see his face. If it was Vardan, she'd have no choice but to save him. But if it was that fool boy from the village, back again...

With a mighty heave and a groan of her own, Briska managed to turn the man face-up.

His eyes drifted open and the dreamiest smile lit his face. "My queen," he croaked. "Finally, I have found you."

Briska's heart stopped. She couldn't even draw breath. It couldn't be. He couldn't be. The Sultan had executed him more than twenty years ago, and she'd looked for him in the mirror every day since. Yet he didn't appear to have aged a day since she last saw him.

"Amani?"

But his eyes had closed again, and his face was turning as blue as his fingers. She had to get him inside, and warm. She hadn't found him after all this time just to lose him again to a bit of snow.

Briska hooked her arms under his armpits and began to haul him home.

Forty-One

Briska managed to get Amani onto the bed once occupied by that young fool, Kai, but she had no idea how to help him. She needed to warm him, or send him into an enchanted sleep like Kai until she could heal him, but her magic refused to cooperate. No matter what spell she tried, she couldn't conjure so much as a spark.

She would have to do things the mundane way, she guessed.

Briska bundled up every blanket and item of clothing she had, and tucked them around

Amani, hoping to preserve what body warmth he still had. Next, she headed outside to find the woodpile, buried under the snow. She couldn't remember the last time she'd built a fire, so she had to dig deep before she found the topmost logs.

She carried them inside, then went back for more, until she had a healthy pyre piled up in the fire pit. She lit it from the lamp, but the tinder caught too slowly, smoking sulkily instead of blazing into eager life. Swearing, Briska opened the lamp and tipped the oil onto the wood. Then the fire caught, licking at kindling and logs alike as it greedily drank the oil.

Briska dropped the lamp on the floor, for it was useless now.

What else did ordinary people use to heal someone who'd come this close to freezing?

A fire, warm clothes and blankets, and conserving their body heat. Or sharing it.

Briska slipped out of her clothes, then slid into bed beside Amani. His skin was cold to the touch – even colder than hers! – but she rubbed against him, trying to share what little warmth she had. A good lust spell would come in really handy right now. Not that she needed it. Just touching him again was enough to kindle her desire. It had been more than twenty years since she'd last touched him, but she remembered every line, every ridge of muscle, like it was yesterday.

She covered his face with kisses, then bit her lip to cast a lust spell. Knowing it would not work, but wishing with all her might to feel his hands on her body one last time.

She kissed and caressed him, her own skin afire at the contact with the man she loved. Against her belly, she felt part of him stirring, though the rest of his body did not. Her fingers strayed lower, stroking him harder until she could bear it no longer.

She climbed atop him, easing the length of him inside her until she could hold no more. Then she began to rock her hips against him, just as she used to do when they were lovers.

Once, he would stare up at her in wonder, his hands moving to cup her breasts, his lips murmuring endearments before he kissed her, moving within her in a blissful harmony that would bring them the most glorious release.

But now…

Briska blinked away tears, wishing for what could never be again.

Behind her, unnoticed, the lamp's light went out.

<h1 style="text-align:center">Forty-Two</h1>

Amani debated whether he was dreaming, or if he'd died and attained paradise, for there was no way Briska could be truly sitting astride him, riding him hard in the pursuit of her own pleasure, as she sent him inexorably to his own glorious peak.

He reached up to cup those glorious breasts, bouncing as she rocked. But there was blood on his hands, and the dimly remembered pain of tearing his palms free of the ice. But blood could cast magic. He sent a powerful healing spell through his body, gritting his teeth against the pain as his ribs knitted together and his hands became whole once more. Only then did he place reverent hands on Briska's hips, wanting to touch her to see if she was real.

Her eyes flew open. "Amani?"

He managed a smile. "You mistook me for some other lover? My queen, you wound me."

"I have no other lover. Never. Not in all this time…"

He rose up, so that he might kiss her lips while still driving deep inside her. Bliss, the like of which he never thought he'd feel again.

"Then you have been neglected for too long. It will take me weeks to make up for my absence. I will make you never want to leave your bed, my queen. For I know I have no wish to leave it." He thrust gently, changing the angle until she gasped. He fixed his gaze on her face as he pushed her to heights of pleasure no one else could reach, and was rewarded by the sound of her screaming his name. At last.

His pleasure could wait. For Briska was and forever would be his queen, and nothing mattered more than bringing a smile to her face, a sigh to her lips, and an enormous, shuddering orgasm that engulfed her completely.

Forty-Three

Briska cried out again, her voice hoarse for the first time in too long. And still Amani played her body until it sang, just for him. She'd lost count of the number of times he'd carried her to that lofty peak of pleasure that made her scream, for once he'd reached it, he started again, just as lovingly as the first time.

"Stop fucking that man!"

Kun's icy tone cut through Briska's pleasure, freezing her in place.

"Now pick up that lamp, and hold it in your hands. He is the slave of the lamp, and as long as you are holding it, you are his mistress. Hold it in your hands and order him to throw himself off the nearest cliff!"

Briska winced as Amani slid out of her, wishing she could disobey the order, but even the thought of trying made her head pound. Blindly, she groped for the lamp.

"Go ahead. You're too late for that," Amani said. He rose from the bed, so that both Briska and Kun could see his naked magnificence, and folded his arms across his chest.

Briska touched the lamp, now cold from lying unlit on the floor for so long, and cradled it in her hands. She didn't want to do this. She didn't. Yet her mouth opened and the words came out anyway, followed by a sob.

And the sound of smashing glass.

Blood trickled down the surface of the mirror, tinting Kun's horrified face red.

"Blood of the betrayed that binds this djinn, set her free!" Amani commanded.

All of a sudden, a weight lifted off Briska, as though she'd been carrying a heavy load that had almost crushed her. The fog in her head – fog she'd scarcely noticed until now – cleared, and she became aware of just how cold she was, standing naked in a palace made of ice.

"NO!" Kun screamed.

"Yes," Amani replied. He flicked his fingers at her. "Now, you will leave us alone, for if I ever see you again, you will not live to see the next day."

Amid a storm of cursing, Kun vanished from the mirror.

"Did you kill the Sultan?" Briska asked, wrapping her arms around herself to try and stay warm. But the very thought of Amani – the man she loved – killing anyone, chilled her heart.

"No, of course not. That blood came from Maram."

"You killed my daughter?" Briska shrieked. She sank her teeth into her lip, determined to curse Amani into oblivion for hurting Maram, but nothing happened. "What is wrong with me?" She rushed at Amani and pummelled him with her fists. "What have you done to me? To her?"

He grasped her wrists and gently pushed her back. "I've made love to you, to the best of my ability. And I have done nothing to Princess Maram that she did not ask for."

Briska snatched up the lamp again. This time, she said the words of her own free will. "I order you to go jump off a cliff and never touch me again."

Instead of obeying, Amani laughed. "If it is your wish, I will not touch you. Because it is your wish. I am no longer a slave, and I have your daughter to thank for it. So do you, for she gave me the vial of her blood and commanded me to use it to free you. Until she told me, I had no idea that you still lived. The moment I was free, I did everything within my power to find you. Now I have…and you are free. No more orders, ever. Least of all from that whore, Kun."

Briska took this all in, looking for a lie, yet knowing she wouldn't find one. His words explained everything, and they even made sense. All except one thing. "But why isn't my magic working?"

His brow furrowed. "I do not know. If you permit me to touch you, perhaps I can find out."

Briska stepped into the circle of his outstretched arms, and breathed a sigh of relief as his warmth engulfed her.

He stood silent for a long moment, before he finally said, "Your magic is working fine. If anything, it's stronger than it ever was. This castle is absolutely humming with it. Every inch of ice and snow, obedient to your command, woven into a protection spell so powerful no one could see through it. Not even to search for you."

"But Kun said...she said she cast the spell. I didn't. I know I didn't. I would have remembered..."

"For a spell of this strength, it would have taken a lot of blood. No wonder she managed to hide you from me for so long. If she cast the initial spell, then used your blood to enhance it...but the amount of blood this would have taken...I don't know how you survived, my queen. Unless she took a little at a time, every day..."

The truth dawned on Briska so suddenly she gasped. She had not thought so quickly in years. "Gerda. When she and the boy stabbed me, I feared I would bleed to death. The floor was awash…and when I awoke it was gone. Kun saved me, or so I thought." She grimaced. "How do I break the spell so that it no longer uses up all my magic?"

"Just let it go," Amani said.

"Let it go?" she asked doubtfully. Breaking spells was usually far more complex than that.

Amani's arms closed around her, his voice a sultry whisper in her ear. "Feel the spell, just as you feel this." His lips kissed her neck, sending a flood of warmth deep into her body. "Then release it."

It was hard to focus, when all she wanted to do was return his kisses and caresses with a few of her own, but Briska did her best. Reaching deep within her to the magic in her blood, she found the spell, a delicate web of threads that radiated out of her and into every facet of the castle. Now she could feel the magic pulsing through the walls of the palace, keeping the world out. No more.

Briska severed the connection.

Magic boiled through her veins, like a flood unleashed on a dry river bed. She bit her lip, and cast the barest whisper of a lust spell.

The power of it swirled around her, more powerful than any blizzard. Swirled around both of them, as desire darkened Amani's eyes.

"My queen, I'm taking you home. My castle is yours, and right now, we need a bed, or my desire will melt this castle the moment I kiss you," he said roughly, tracing a circle in the air.

Lifting Briska in his arms, Amani stepped through the portal, from icy mountain to searing desert. No, not just the desert. A castle in the desert, and he was already carrying her inside.

Briska laughed. Inside, the castle was bare, but she had magic to spare. She conjured a bed, big enough to fit a sultan and a dozen concubines, then squealed as Amani tossed her on top of the silk cushions.

He fell to his knees on the end of the bed. "Permit me to love you, my queen. Every day for the rest of my life. Be my wife, and I shall worship you every night for as long as I live."

"Yes," she whispered as Amani took her in his arms, sliding between her legs and deep within her. "Yes!" And she melted under his touch, just the way she wanted. She was the snow queen no more.

199

Forty-Four

Kun stepped out of her portal, pulling her cloak more closely around her thin frame. There was no sign of the accursed couple, or the magic that had once protected this icy palace from the elements. Already the wall beside the waterfall had collapsed into the river, letting snow into the chambers where Briska had hidden from the world for so long.

Kun sighed. She would never find another matchmaker as talented as Briska. The girl had a gift for finding precisely the right moment to cast her spell, weaving the couples together so closely they never even suspected. She would have liked to keep the girl for longer, for her work was nowhere near done, but that damned enchanter had ruined everything. She still didn't know how he'd managed to free himself from servitude, or to free Briska, but it served him right. He'd thrown away immortality to rut like rabbits with the little matchmaker queen. So stupid. But so were most men, when they thought with their pricks. Centuries had passed, but men never changed.

She stepped into the palace, trudging through the blown snow, until she reached the mirror. A thin layer of blood crusted the glass, but that could be cleaned off. She would take the mirror back to her palace in the floating city, where it belonged. It had served her purpose, and so had Briska.

She'd pushed Molina and Lubos together, ensuring they produced a child, and she'd even dealt with that dreadful scion of House Rumpelstiltskin. And with Briska doing all the matchmaking, she'd left Kun free to tend to the training of Molina's daughter, and to do it properly.

Grasping the mirror, Kun stepped back through the portal. She would return it to her palace later, when Molina's daughter was asleep.

"Good day, Mother," Rapunzel said.

Not that the girl knew she was Molina's daughter, of course.

Kun smiled. "It is, isn't it? The future looks quite rosy, now I have you."

Rapunzel looked puzzled, but still she smiled. "Yes, Mother."

Yes, the future looked rosy indeed, though it could darken as much as Kun desired, for now she had Rapunzel, she could weave whatever fate she wanted.

About the Author

Demelza Carlton has always loved the ocean, but on her first snorkelling trip she found she was afraid of fish.

She has since swum with sea lions, sharks and sea cucumbers and stood on spray drenched cliffs over a seething sea as a seven-metre cyclonic swell surged in, shattering a shipwreck below.

Demelza now lives in Perth, Western Australia, the shark attack capital of the world.

The *Ocean's Gift* series was her first foray into fiction, followed by her suspense thriller *Nightmares* trilogy. She swears the *Mel Goes to Hell* series ambushed her on a crowded train and wouldn't leave her alone.

Want to know more? You can follow Demelza on Facebook, Twitter, YouTube or her website, Demelza Carlton's Place at:

www.demelzacarlton.com

Books by Demelza Carlton

Ocean's Gift series
Ocean's Gift (#1)
Ocean's Infiltrator (#2)
Ocean's Depths (#3)
Water and Fire

Turbulence and Triumph series
Ocean's Justice (#1)
Ocean's Trial (#2)
Ocean's Triumph (#3)
Ocean's Ride (#4)
Ocean's Cage (#5)
Ocean's Birth (#6)
How To Catch Crabs

Nightmares Trilogy
Nightmares of Caitlin Lockyer (#1)
Necessary Evil of Nathan Miller (#2)
Afterlife of Alana Miller (#3)

The Complex series
Halcyon
Fishtail

Mel Goes to Hell series

Welcome to Hell (#1)
See You in Hell (#2)
Mel Goes to Hell (#3)
To Hell and Back (#4)
The Holiday From Hell (#5)
All Hell Breaks Loose (#6)

Romance Island Resort series

Maid for the Rock Star (#1)
The Rock Star's Email Order Bride (#2)
The Rock Star's Virginity (#3)
The Rock Star and the Billionaire (#4)
The Rock Star Wants A Wife (#5)
The Rock Star's Wedding (#6)
Maid for the South Pole (#7)
Jailbird Bride (#8)

Romance a Medieval Fairytale series

Enchant: Beauty and the Beast Retold
Dance: Cinderella Retold
Fly: Goose Girl Retold
Revel: Twelve Dancing Princesses Retold
Silence: Little Mermaid Retold
Awaken: Sleeping Beauty Retold
Embellish: Brave Little Tailor Retold
Appease: Princess and the Pea Retold
Blow: Three Little Pigs Retold
Return: Hansel and Gretel Retold
Wish: Aladdin Retold
Melt: Snow Queen Retold